Ellipsis

An Anthology of Humorous Short Stories

Table of Contents

Introduction by Lisa Shiroff   9

Joseph Ferguson, *My Favorite Christmas Tree*   13

Lisa Shiroff, *Mai Tai Mediation*   19

G. H. Neale, *En la Plaza Mayor*   37

Mileva Anastasiadou, *The 12 Hits of Christmas*   49

Barry Parham, *Equally Cold Calls*   67

Hema Nataraju, *Shave*   75

Brena Mercer, *Dirty, Dirty, Dirty Money*   79

Don Ake, *I Went Hunting in the Bushlands*   85

Dylan Callens, *The Splooge Jar*   91

Shoshanah Lee Marohn, *Piano Camp*   99

Meaghan Curley, *The CARF Crisis*   115

Hákon Gunnarsson, *The Ballad of the Fire Spewing Dragon*   133

Elaine Fields Smith, *Six at Six*   145

Mehreen Ahmed, *Charade*   149

Melinda Tarcon, *The Great Iced-Coffee Catastrophe*   183

G. Allen Cook, *No Easy Trick*   199

Peter Marino, *My Stepfather, The Hawk*   205

Introduction

When great minds come together, something amazing inevitably happens. Diseases are cured. New worlds are discovered. Great problems are solved. Peanut butter and jelly are joined to make sandwich bliss.

When comedic minds come together, something altogether different happens. You get this: an anthology of seventeen short stories that promise to delight, inspire, and educate you—or at least make you groan in discomfort.

What may be of interesting note is that while the stories in this volume cross most genres, are written in a wide range of styles, vary in length and structure, and are composed by writers who had never met each other, there is an underlying common thread uniting them. That is, life lessons abound! How, you wonder? In ways only a comic can imagine.

For example, you will find two Christmas stories. In "My Favorite Christmas Tree," Joseph Ferguson reminds us that it is never wise to be the first among your friends to pass out while drinking. Then in "The Twelve Hits of Christmas," Mileva Anastasiadou warns you about what happens if you habitually don't heed Joseph's advice.

Lest you think this book is only about Yule-tide boozing it up, please be assured serious and mature topics are also covered. In fact a few stories offer words of wisdom regarding your career. Dylan Callens reminds us in "The Splooge Jar," that if all else fails, look to the internet for a healthy pay day. And in Hákon Gunnarsson's "The Ballad of the Fire-Spewing Dragon" we're warned against becoming so complacent in our jobs that we don't keep our resumes up to date.

Direct and practical advice comes to us by way of Barry Parham, who provides a transcript for properly dealing with telemarketers in "Equally Cold Calls." Meghan Curley depicts a plan of action for handling Fan Girl extremists in "The CARF Crisis." And Elaine Smith assures us in "Six at Six" that aging gracefully is easier if you have a good friend by your side.

Some of the life lessons found between these covers come from stories based on bad ideas. In fact, both Shoshanah Lee Marohn's "Piano Camp" and Hema Natarajan's "Shave" offer examples for why it's necessary to think twice about the company you're about to keep.

Speaking of good company, or bad, Brena Mercer reminds us in "Dirty, Dirty, Dirty Money" that regardless of how weird you think the folks around you are, there is at least one thing that you share in common with them. Similarly, Mehreen Ahmed's "Charades" focuses on how people appear versus being their real selves.

Of course how to choose a good mate is a life lesson most of us would like to learn via osmosis, but instead often learn from experience. Regardless, a few of the authors here are trying to prevent you from making too big of a mistake. To that end, Melinda Tarcon, in "The Great Iced-Coffee Catastrophe," shows you how marital bliss is possible despite the stress from extreme adverse conditions. Don Ake is proof positive that it's not just appliances that wives resent for their birthdays in "I Went Hunting in the Bushlands." G. H. Neale offers up a Joycean discourse in "En la Plaza Mayor" where he shows us couples bonding over their casual observation of others. And perhaps to bring the book full-circle and get back to drinking again, I peddle hope for second chances in "Mai Tai Mediation."

Finally, the book ends with G. Allen Cook's warning to be careful for what you wish for in "No Easy Trick," and fatherly love in Peter Marino's, "My Stepfather, The Hawk."

The overall goal of the book is to offer a glimpse of the world through the humorist's eye. According to John Vorhaus, "comedy is truth and pain." It is only because humans share in common painful experiences from the, sometimes sad, reality of their lives that they are able to laugh. Often, it takes a comic to help us find that laughter. To wit: this book.

A final note: the authors who contributed to this volume come from around the globe. Some write in American English, others in British English. Still others are writing in English as a second language to them. Hence, you will find a variety of grammar, word usage and even some spelling that may seem a little off to you. Please look beyond it, sit back and just enjoy the story.

Thank you,
Lisa Shiroff

Joseph Ferguson

Joseph Ferguson is an author, poet, and journalist appearing in a variety of small press, regional, and national publications. He also wrote propaganda for a variety of entities for some 25 years. His recent collection of short fiction, *Southbound*, follows the exploits of one character, Basement Man.

He is a former editor and critic for Hudson Valley , ran the Fiction Workshop for the Poughkeepsie Library District, and regularly reviews books and videos for Climbing, The American Book Review, Kirkus Indie, and a number of other publications.

His new short story collection, *Shillelagh Law and Other Stories*, will be available this fall. Check his Amazon author page for further information.

Author Page: https://www.amazon.com/Joseph-Ferguson/e/B01E672FQ4/ref=dp_byline_cont_ebooks_1
Check out *Southbound* on Amazon: https://www.amazon.com/dp/B0184SEI8O
He also sells rock climbing t-shirts through his website: http://www.bumluckhome.com/

My Favorite Christmas Tree

The names in this story are true.

Only the facts have been changed.

None are innocent.

We called ourselves the Scurvy Bastards. To us, drinking was science; the weekend our laboratory; our bodies, test tubes; and our minds, the experiment.

Every Friday and Saturday, each of us would absorb three to four times the lethal dose of alcohol, and have others report back on our actions. Needless to say, this was fascinating research.

One night, whilst sitting on the Scurvy Benches, as was our wont, the Electrician (a man permanently wired) had just dismissed the whole of Kant's epistemology with the words, "That faggot didn't even drink."

The air was crisp as lettuce and miniature fogs arose whenever someone used the Pissing Tree. The Electrician's irrefutable logic set Feeney thinking. Feeney did a great deal of thinking. He had to. No one could be that disturbed or disturbing without having put a great deal of thought into it. He was something of an enigma wrapped in legend. None knew from whence he came; he would appear like some mythical being, gym bag filled with books, Jameson, and Stout, dressed like Sherlock Holmes. He had a great red beard, and spoke in parables. One night he passed out and we found the only identification he bore was a membership card to the Dudley Do-Right fan club in the name of Little Bobby Feeney.

At present, Feeney was engaged in what he termed, "The Great Experiment." The premise was as simple as it was ingenious: How long can a human being subsist on Guinness Stout and Cheese Doodles? Feeney was determined to learn the answer.

"Hey Josh." Feeney referred to everyone as Josh for no discernible reason. "Hey Josh; do you think James Joyce could have drunk the same amount that killed Dylan Thomas without croaking?" Here was a question of comparative literature we had not before considered. Speculation was rampant.

"I ... could." The words dropped from Hose's mouth with the finality of a coffin lid falling. Already six sheets to the wind, Hose hugged his wine bottle as a child does a stuffed toy. He swayed in the slight breeze, not as ordinary drunken men, but with a lizard-like slowness, quite remarkable to behold.

"Fuck you!" The response was instant and unanimous.

"I ... could." No change in tone; a simple reiteration of fact, repeated merely for our edification. We could believe it; or we could go to hell.

Hose was a drunk's drunk. If necessary, he could swill chemical waste. He passed out with his eyes open. He could piss for hours (hence, the Hose), and it was rumored the mighty Pissing Tree was but a sapling before Hose drank in the park.

Feeney knew, or claimed to know, the exact dosage in question; as well as how long Hose had to complete this task. He produced a fresh bottle of Jameson 12-year-old. "You have 20 minutes to drink this, Josh." Feeney's wide theatrical wink was so evident, only someone drunk as Hose could have missed it.

Within minutes, Hose snored loudly at the sky while we drank not only the Jameson, but his wine to boot.

It was a long-standing tradition among the Bastards to treat fallen comrades as blank canvasses; tabulae rasae, if you will, to be filled with dream and fancy.

When the Nut passed out, we colored his wrists with Mercurochrome and bandage, telling him he tried to slit them in a drunken fury. When the Electrician passed out (a rare occasion) we deposited him in front of a VFW meeting, tied to a bicycle, a brick on his chest, with Marxist slogans inscribed on his face and hands. I myself, awoke one morning astride a police cruiser wearing "off the pigs" placards.

What could we do with our latest victim? Feeney, who had recently inherited money, suggested we empty Hose's pockets and put him on a plane to London. This, naturally, met with great approval, until we realized he would never be allowed on a plane. Other suggestions, which ranged from putting honey in his hair under a bees' nest, to placing him in a various bar denominations tattooed with the appropriate inappropriate watchwords, were all vetoed; largely because they involved leaving the park.

Finally, seeing as it was nearly Christmas, we decided it might be nice to decorate him. Besides, he was already lit, so to speak. At any rate, it wouldn't have to be fancy; just materials at hand.

Everyone was filled with the holiday spirit. Empty beer cans were restrung into their plastic wrappers and draped festively from his ears. Bottles were attached by their necks to each of his fingers. Old wads of chewing gum were stuck to his face. The Nut festively strewed bits of paper about him, while old napkins were stuffed in his nose. His pockets were filled with rocks, dirt, and dead insects, while his entire body was dusted with a fine coat of sand. For the top piece, a water fountain was torn from its stand and placed on his head.

He was beautiful. There was no getting around it; the Hose was beautiful. We had truly outdone ourselves, and there was talk of bringing him to the Guggenheim; but we dared not disturb our work. The fountain caught the magic play of streetlights, crowning him with a halo. The bottles resembled Robert-the-Robot fingers, while the beer cans swayed like great Raggedy Ann curls. Even the sand glistened with the spirit of the season and seemed to capture the starlight itself.

The Electrician giggled and gamboled, dancing like an unearthly sprite through the gnarled shadows of trees and the misty wash of the park lights. The Nut, blinded by tears of joy, ran straight into the Pissing Tree.

Still ... there was something missing.

Feeney stood back and eyed the Hose for a long time. "Hey Josh," he said finally to no one in particular, "Hand me that gallon wine jug and his shoe laces.

Sensing something big was about to happen, the Electrician stopped in mid gambol, the Nut's tears dried, and we all gathered slowly about the Hose like zombies in a corn field.

Without a word, Feeney took the bottle and string and moved toward the Hose with the deliberation of a surgeon. The Hose's pants seemed to come off by magic and there sat his privates like a dead bird on the cold wooden bench. The silence grew deeper. The lights in the park seemed to dim; and the whole world seemed a View-Master scene.

At last, with a flourish such as Dali must give daubing the last stroke; Feeney slid the mouth of the bottle over Hose's hose, securing it to his legs with the laces.

The silence grew for one last moment before Feeney and the Electrician, as if moved by one thought, let out howls from some primitive depths long dormant in the human species.

Beer cans were strung into maracas, garbage cans became drums, wine bottles - flutes. Round and round him we danced hooting, chanting, and rattling our cans in a wild Druidic rite of winter.

As we moved, the winds picked up, undulating the bony branches of the Pissing Tree, which moaned in mournful unison to our song. Shadows squirmed on the ground, as monolithic clouds began to cross before the moon.

Dogs howled. Cats screeched. The cops came.

As we ran for the compass points, I heard one muffled "oof," as Hose tried to scratch himself with a glass finger.

Lisa Shiroff

Lisa Shiroff is a comedic fiction writer celebrating the often unnoticed but beautifully bizarre in life. For years, she worked professionally as a corporate freelance writer and graphic designer. Not only can she Photoshop her way into a royal wedding, but she can write a PR piece that will make a cat in a tattered wolf costume sound like a Westminster Dog Show champion. But when the struggle to keep her tongue out of her cheek gave her TMJ symptoms, she decided she'd had enough. It was time she joined the ranks of those intent on using humor to balance out the negatives in the universe. Now she is unleashing her comedic perspective on anyone willing to take the risk to read whatever she writes.

Having spent her formative years in small-town America, Lisa mastered the ability to amuse herself and others with tales about people we all wished lived next door (and some who really did). Now she's bringing those stories to light in novels with funny characters experiencing sometimes inane circumstances and always finding happy endings (yes, she's a sucker for them).

Almost living the American Dream, Lisa lives in south Jersey with her husband, two kids, and a dog. Alas, she has no picket fence.

Lisa can be found at www.LisaShiroff.com and www.tinyurl.com/amazonLisaShiroff or you can stalk her on Facebook (https://www.facebook.com/lisa.shiroff.9) and Twitter (@LisaShiroff). Yes, Oscar Wilde had a point when he said "Consistency is the last resort of the unimaginative," but that was because no one was a "brand" back then.

Mai Tai Mediation

When Nate first researched how to make the classic Mai Tai, he found it ironic that despite having a Tahitian word for a name, the drink was originally created with Jamaican rum. Later, as he experimented to perfect his own recipe, he found it ironic when he learned it was the most requested drink by tourists in Hawaii, even though it was invented in California. So perhaps it's no surprise that when his wife said his Mai Tais were what destroyed their marriage, Nate found it ironic. After all, everyone knew the real culprit was some guy named Derek.

Regardless of the ironies, or maybe because of them, Nate dedicated his post-divorce life to the appreciation of the Mai Tai. And to be sure he got the last word, he moved to Ecuador in what only he considered a final ironic gesture: he would have failed Spanish back in college if his then-girlfriend-now-ex-wife hadn't let him cheat off of her.

To be precise, Nate wound up living and working at a small, ocean-side, eco-friendly resort seventeen miles north of the Equator in the Manabi province. Along with his best bud Lou, he owned half the resort. The other half was owned by a local millionaire agricultural exporter who was waiting, impatiently, for the American ex-pats to earn enough money to completely buy him out.

Not that earnings were ever in the forefront of Nate's mind. Lou looked after the finances. Nate contented himself by working with his hands: touching up paint, securing hammocks, and occasionally shoving that damn pipe in the pool pump back into place. Outside of that, he continued his quest to find the perfect rum to create the perfect Mai Tai.

At the end of each day, Nate would reward himself for doing a good job. He'd head to the resort's outdoor bar, a large Tiki hut strung and lit by holiday lights, and make himself his favored drink. He'd hoist the glass high and encourage all the tourists within earshot to toast his ex-wife with him.

"Jimmy Buffet was wrong," he'd say. "It *was* the woman's fault."

Often, by Mai Tai number four, Nate would forget about the arthritis pre-maturely setting up in his back and lumber down to the wooden lounge chairs lined up on the beach. There, under a thatched canopy just out of reach of high tide, he'd cover himself with a towel and sip his drink until his eyes closed without him realizing it.

It was after such a four-Tai night when Nate was lured awake by a familiar sound. At first it came to him on the breeze, sweetly enfolding his chest with a nostalgic warmth. But as it neared, it morphed into a searing burn, something more akin to the sensation of a hot knife rammed between his ribs. It was a sound that, had he believed in a god, he would have prayed never to hear again.

"Good morning, sunshine." High-pitched and gentle, yet with an edge that hinted at raw punk, the sound by his side was a clone of his ex-wife's voice. Nate opened his eyes and briefly contemplated joining a church. Maybe he had been too hasty on giving up that prayer thing because there stood Eve, the woman he no longer happily called his own. Lou was behind her, eyes bulging as he tugged at the neck of his faded T-shirt.

"Uh, yeah." Lou visibly swallowed. "Nate, look, Eve's here."

"So she is," Nate said.

"And so are you," Eve said. She placed one hand on her hip and tapped her chin with the other. "Sleeping on the beach. Is this your home? It's cute but what about when it rains?"

Nate rolled away from her and grunted. "It's not rainy season." He gingerly forced himself upright, planting his feet on the sand, keeping his back to his ex-wife. "Ugh, errgh." He squeezed his shoulder blades together. "And if it were rainy season, I'd have slept in a hammock under the Tiki bar, Eve. I'm not an idiot, you know."

"So you say."

Ignoring her, Nate pressed his palms against the lounge for leverage and slowly stood. An image of the hot little number who teaches yoga at the resort entered his mind's eye. He could almost hear her honeyed voice telling the class to stand up . . . slowly . . . one . . . vertebra . . . at a time. "Ow. Oh!" He made it: he was completely vertical.

"I guess the Tropics didn't turn out to be a cure all, huh?" Eve walked around the lounge to face him.

"What do you want, Eve?" he growled.

"A tour." She cocked an eyebrow. "What else?"

"What?" Shuffling his feet in the sand to find his flip flops, Nate's toe touched a glass from the night before. He winced. It would take him a minute or two, maybe even three, to pick that baby up. Which was bad enough. Knowing Eve would watch his body resist moving the way her young lover's easily could, was almost too much to deal with. He almost returned to his lounge to snooze a little while longer, but he had a feeling she'd just wait for him to wake up again. "What do you mean?" he asked.

"Let's start at the Tiki bar," Eve said. She spun on her heel as best she could in the sand and sauntered toward the bar. A large tote bag was slung over a shoulder and a pair of pointy heeled sandals dangled from a hand.

He shook his head and sighed. He'd have to follow her. Not because he desired her company. He desired the Bloody Mary the bartender, Albaro, would have waiting for him. But first, he'd have to pick up that damned glass.

"Lou." He turned around and discovered he was alone. He wasn't surprised. Lou was a true pacifist with a strong disliking of violence of any sort. Nate guessed he took shelter from the imminent verbal hurricane that his ex-spouse was so good at churning up within him.

23

Eve was already sipping a mimosa when finally Nate managed to climb on a stool as far from her as possible.

"*Hola* General," Alvaro greeted him. "*Aqui.* Breakfast!" He set a Bloody Mary, complete with a fresh celery stick, in front of Nate.

"General?" Eve called as she came over. "You have them call you *General*?" She sat on the stool next to him.

"You have no sense of humor so you won't get this, but," Nate paused to sip. "When we first got here, someone asked me what I used to do for a living. I explained I ran a bunch of general hardware stores. They had no idea what I was talking about but someone else asked since Lou said to be called *Lou*, did that mean he was my lieutenant." He shrugged.

"I have a sense of humor." She took along slug of her mimosa before tilting her glass toward him. "That's only mildly amusing."

They finished their liquid breakfasts in silence. Nate spent the time speculating on why she was there. It seemed she had traveled alone. Did she come to win him back? Did he want her to want him back? Or was he just contemplating that because her cleavage seemed almost impossible to ignore. Eve never underestimated the power of a good pushup bra.

He rotated on his stool and stared at the Pacific Ocean thinking it was most likely that she came down to see what kind of money he was earning to take an even bigger slice of his pie. He'd have to force that coward Lou to deal with her.

24

By the time both glasses were empty, Nate had forgotten her cleavage long enough that he'd begun toying with the idea of going to his cabana to sleep off the morning. Eve, apparently, had other plans.

"I'm ready." She slid off her stool.

"For what?" His eyes followed her backside as she returned to her original seat.

"My tour." She wiped the sand off her feet, slipped into her stilettos with grace, and straightened to look at him with one eyebrow cocked in anticipation.

A full minute went by in silence. Nate watched as a smile spread over Eve's face. The kind of smile a deceitful little girl uses while playing innocent as she sets up her brother up for lighting Grandma's house on fire. Nate's grizzled face remained impassive even though he had a feeling he was at the wrong end of a punch line.

"Very good. I'll lead," Eve eventually announced. "You can tell me what's what." Once more, she walked away from him.

And once more, Nate had to follow her. He was, after all, heading to his cabana to go back to bed, and she happened to be going in the same direction, walking in front of him.

Alvaro's bartender ESP kicked in. He handed Nate another Bloody Mary without being asked. Nate tossed the celery aside and glugged down half before going to Eve. That is, before going to his cabana. It's just that Eve had stopped and was waiting for him by the pool.

"Why are all those people there in the corner?" She pointed toward a motley group of tourists, employees, and what was probably some locals gathered around a few tables pushed together on the pool deck. "Do you have activities?"

"We do, but not there. That's where Wi-Fi reception is best."

"Hmm."

She wove her way along the stone path separating the main building from the top-of-the-line bungalows. Nate remained mute, sipping his Bloody Mary as he trudged behind her, trying not to stare at her ass. He'd always liked that ass.

They made it about halfway around the compound before Eve stopped again.

"What the hell?" She pulled Nate in front of her, as if she expected him to serve as a shield.

"Those are cows." Nate stepped aside so she would be exposed to the longhorns should one go rogue. "I'm sure you've heard of cows before."

"I have, professor. But what are they doing at the resort? Is the restaurant's beef that fresh?"

"Actually, it is. But it doesn't come from those cows." Nate waved at a middle-aged man on a quad ATV.

"Who's he?"

"The cow herder."

"And he herds his cows on resort property?"

"Sometimes cows go where they want to go. He'll get them back where they belong soon enough."

"Hmm," she said again.

Nate found the *hmm* answers unsettling. He wanted to ask what she was thinking, because each *hmm* sounded to him like she was calculating something in her pretty blond head. A calculation he probably did not want to learn the sum of for as long as possible.

They rounded the back of the main building where the high-end bungalows gave way to the regular cabanas. Nate intentionally slipped farther and farther behind her. When he reached his cabana, she was nearing the section of the path that would force her to make a dogleg left and put him out of her sight. She would be able to see the ocean from there so she wouldn't get lost finding her way back to wherever she wanted to go. Not that he cared if she got lost, he told himself. He tried to believe he just didn't want to miss his nap, which he'd have to do in order to get the authorities involved in finding her body.

As it turned out, it didn't matter what she could or could not see because she easily heard his keys jingling when he attempted to unlock his door. One of the things Nate had yet to do, aside from getting new piping for the pool pump, was to change out the old keyed locks for electronic card ones. Truthfully, he hadn't even started on that project because it had never seemed to be the imminent need it now was.

"What's this?" she asked upon approach.

"My daytime home." He pushed the door open. "I'm done being tour guide now. Good-bye." He saluted her and turned to go inside. She stayed on his heels, keeping too close for him to shut the door on her.

"Where's your tattoo?" she asked.

"Huh?" Nate faced her.

"Your tattoo. Where is it?" She breezed past him to drop her tote bag on his neatly made bed with the state-of-the-art, no-pressure-points mattress.

Only ice remained in his glass. He pressed it against his forehead, suddenly worried he was feverish and hallucinating. Granted, he was in a low-risk area for malaria, and he was one of those rare people who were never bitten by mosquitoes, but hallucinations could explain so much at the moment.

"You do have one, right?" she continued.

"Well, um, no."

"But you are planning on it, aren't you?" With an almost violent tug, she ripped open a curtain. Sunlight blazed in with a similar tinge of hostility. "I mean," she continued without letting him answer, "you're living in a bamboo hut with a thatched roof. There's a hammock right outside your door. The only thing missing is a tattoo." She ran her hand over the bright red and yellow bed cover before looking up at him with a slight snarl on her face. "I bet you even got a sweet Chiquita who pretends not to notice your hair is thinning."

Nate instinctively touched the back of his head. "Fuck you," he said when he realized what he was doing. "And get out!" He swept his arm toward the door.

Eve didn't budge. "You got the life, huh?"

"I don't know." He sighed and sat on a rattan chair next to a table that was so small he didn't think the word *dinette* would even apply to it. Not for the first time did he wish he kept Bloody Mary mix and vodka in his equally small fridge. "It depends. Was that a *huh* or a *hmm*?"

"What?"

"What do you want from me? How the hell did you even find me?"

"I didn't find you. Daddy did."

"Ah, I see," Nate nodded. "The old forensic accountant tried to find more money for you, eh? What a lucky daughter you are."

"Yes, I am lucky to have my dad. But he actually helped me find a way to spend some money."

"Funny. I always thought you were good at that."

"You're such a shit sometimes, you know that?" She shook her hair away from her face. "I didn't come all this way to fight with you, Nate."

"Too bad because I'd like to go a few rounds with you."

"Will you stop being an asshole for two seconds?"

"Will you stop calling me names?"

"Will you stop acting like someone who deserves to be called a name?"

"Well, if that's the rule, then listen here you bitch, slut, whore—"

"Stop!" She held a hand up like a police officer directing traffic. "Whore, I do not deserve." She gave him a crooked smile. He couldn't help but smirk back at her. "Ask me *why* I'm here, Nate. That's the question I'm waiting for."

"I don't think I want to know, but I'll bite." Nate paused as he stared, longingly, into his empty glass before looking up at her, coldly. "Why are you here?"

She examined her manicure before answering. For some reason, she had to lean back on the bed and stretch out her legs while she did it. Nate thought she may have even arched her back, too, and he hated himself a little for being turned on by it.

"When Daddy discovered you and Lou only own half this place—"

"Oh, no."

"He also discovered your local partner was willing to sell the other half."

"Oh. Hell. No."

"So I bought it." She plastered the evil-sister smile on her face again.

Nate was mute as she picked up her bag and stood. She kissed him on the forehead and left the cabana.

Late that afternoon, Eve was thoroughly ensconced in a lounge chair by the pool. She tapped away on a laptop computer finally making good on her promise to one day write a novel. In chapter two, she had accidentally killed off the person she had planned to be the murderer, which left her with a bit of a problem. She sat, chewing her bottom lip, wondering how to fix it, when a member of the resort staff approached her.

"*Buenos tardes, señora*." He smiled at her. "The General, he say you Boss Lady now."

"Oh no, not me." Eve shook her head. "I'm a partner with him. That's all. I'm not a boss."

"*Si, si*. Okay." He nodded as if he understood. "The pool pump. She is leaking water again."

Eve waited for him to continue but it appeared he thought he had said enough.

"That's not supposed to happen, is it?" she prompted.

"No."

"Well," she glanced at his name tag, "Danilo, someone should fix it," she offered.

"Right. The General say to tell you."

"Who usually fixes it?"

"The General."

Eve snapped her laptop shut. "Where is the General?" She rose, slowly. Something about her slowness as she gained altitude made Danilo take a step back.

31

"His cabana," he squeaked out.

"Thank you." Eve smiled sweetly at him, not remembering which cabana was Nate's. She took off her wide brimmed hat and tousled her hair. "Can you lead me to him?"

Of course he could.

Nate didn't answer the door when she knocked, but through the window, she could see him packing a suitcase.

She knocked again, louder.

"Nate!" she yelled. "You can't leave unless you go through this door. I'll wait you out."

No reply.

"Yo, Nate!" Lou yelled, rounding the cabana. He locked eyes with Eve and ran off the way he came.

Eve picked up a rock and beat it against the door.

"Fine!" she shouted. "I'll bang on this door all freaking day."

After a full three minutes of her pounding, Nate couldn't take it anymore. He yanked open the door. "What the hell do you want?"

"You to fix the pool thingy," she said with sugar on her tongue.

Instead of answering, he returned to his bed and resumed packing. She breezed in behind him.

"Whatcha doing?" Eve sat beside the suitcase on the bed, squishing his pile of clothes beneath her rear and beamed up at him.

"You were smart enough to track me down. You should be smart enough to figure out I'm packing a suitcase." He tried to pull a pair of swim trunks from under her.

She squirmed harder against the clothes.

"That's right. I forgot," he said. "*Daddy* tracked me down. Well then, let me explain. I'm leaving." With a hard tug, he yanked out the trunks. She toppled over, falling against the suitcase. It crashed to the floor, upside down, spilling all contents.

Nate shook his fists in the air. "I give up!" he shouted. "You win! Again." He threw the swim trunks at her. "Why are you doing this to me? What the hell do you want?"

She removed the trunks from her head, somehow with panache. "Only what you owe me."

"What I owe you?" Instead of slamming a fist against the wall, he paced circles around the tiny table and chairs. "I owe you nothing. You didn't just get half of all I worked for, thanks to good old Daddy, but you got close to everything! *I* could only afford a *quarter* of this place. You bought half."

"You owe me a life, Nate. A married, happily-ever-after life." Her words made him stop.

"We had that." He glared into her. "And you killed it. So now we're both fucked, right?"

"Right." Eve had the audacity to grin. He thought he saw her shoulders relax. It made him want to punch her. "Now, think really hard, Nate. Remember what we used to say back in college?"

"What?"

"What was the standard response when someone said something like 'I'm so fucked'?"

Nate blinked at her, not breathing while he thought. Eventually, he answered. "That they should make sure they got an orgasm out of it."

She full out smiled and nodded. "Right. And that's what I did."

"Yes, I know." The bitterness was back in his voice. "With that Derek dude. On the dining-room table." He couldn't hold himself back any longer. His fist struck the tiny dinette hard enough to make it collapse. "OW!" Tears stung his eyes. "Why am I the one who keeps getting hurt?" he hollered. "For the record, I'm the one who was fucked, you know, and twice by that table. The first time was the fifteen grand you made me spend on it and the second time by the visual still burning in my brain of Derek screwing you on it."

"And I'd been fucked for the previous twenty years, Nate." Eve stood with fists clenched at her side. "Look at the life I lived for you."

"You had everything you wanted!"

"I had everything you wanted to give me, you mean."

"You had a gorgeous fucking house. A veritable mansion in the hills. You had expensive cars! Jewelry! Clothing! My God! I used to think you'd bleed from the ears if you passed a pair of shoes and didn't buy them." Instead of hitting her, and because the table was already a heap of wood, he resumed pacing, making circles around the cabana.

She twirled in slow-motion, watching him as she spoke. "What I wanted, the only thing *I wanted*, was *this*!" She grabbed his arm and made him stop. "This! With you! And that's what you promised me. Remember? When we got married, that was the plan. You would climb the corporate ladder, retire early, and we'd move to the Tropics where we'd run a B&B or something. But instead, you kept climbing. You kept getting transferred so I couldn't even put down roots and create a life of some kind while you worked ALL. THE. FUCKING. TIME."

Nate saw tears in her eyes and had to look away. He'd never been able to handle her tears when sober. He vowed if he stayed at the resort, stocking that damn fridge with booze would be the first thing on the agenda. Second thing, actually, because the pool pump needed to be taken care of first.

But he wasn't staying if she was.

"So you've come to take away my slice of paradise?" he asked.

"Ugh!" She slapped her forehead. "You idiot! Don't you get it?"

"Obviously not." Nate sat on a chair and, elbows on knees, cradled his face in his hands.

She took the other chair on the opposite side of the wood pile that was formerly known as a tiny table.

"When Daddy found you," she said, calmly. "I realized you were living our dream without me. And that wasn't right. It was *our* dream. So I bought out your partner. And I know that once you get over the shock of it, this will make you happy."

"Ha!" Nate threw his head back. "Yes, because I want to be reminded every day of what you put me through. I never knew I was such a masochist. It's a good thing I got you in my corner to keep me focused, babe." He sneered at her.

"During our last day in divorce court, you said I was your one and only. That you could love only me."

"I have no memory of that."

"I'm sure. You passed out right after you said it, but *in vino veritas,* right?"

"And in bourbon, bullshit." Nate stood. "I'm pretty sure that's what I was drinking that day." He grunted as he stooped to pick up his suitcase.

"It doesn't matter," Eve said from close behind him. "We're here now. This is our chance for us both to orgasm."

He turned and met her eyes. He had always hated when she was right. But sometimes she was. And now seemed to be one of those times. He had abandoned the dream and their marriage first.

He sighed and walked toward the door.

"Where are you going?" she asked.

"To shove that god-damned pipe back in the pool pump."

She grinned.

"And then, I'm going out to the bar where I will make a couple of Mai Tais," he said. "If you want to get fucked right, you'll join me on the beach tonight."

G. H. Neale

Mr. G H Neale was born the same week as the death penalty was abolished in the United Kingdom – a matter of some good fortune. He is occasionally accompanied by his wife and three children as he traverses the highways and byways of the Kentish countryside. His favorite author is Flann O'Brien and proudly claims, without any deception, to have read *Finnegans Wake* more than once.

His first novel ARCHIPELAGO received a number of five star reviews on Amazon and elsewhere as well as a superlative review here: http://booksist.net/book-reviews/archipelago-ghneale/. This extract is from his current work-in-progress, ARRIBA. Its contents may change considerably but he presents it to you within this anthology with a fervent expectation that you may cathartically experience joy or unease. Either emotion is worthy; for there is no point in doing things by hum drums and quarters.

He wishes everyone well, except others that don't wish others well.

He appears in pseudonym as Señor Sin Nombre, and from time to time blogs a bit about distressing matters here: http://archipelagoaproblem.blogspot.co.uk/

Investigate his website to keep up to date with his scribblings: www.pmvideos.com or follow him on Twitter @GHNeale

En la Plaza Mayor

A narrow escape through narrow streets which at that time materialised, as Madrileños who were out for the evening, evinced by bodies brushing past all higgledy-piggledy on top of each, seeking sought, hunted, and who were, or who had either in the past sought a-something, strolled and became lit by orange lanterns that reflected in the twinkling evening's dusky-baroqued shadows, embozado, façaded with apricot-titian coloured walls that would seem just as stoned in the morning. Our four heroes explored, paesoed and perambulated: led by eyes, ears, noses but mainly bellies: wandering in wonder and hunger hunting; yet concerned with passing picaros waiting to pick a pocket or four, barbarous tales of Moorish encampments, skeuomorphed swerved and skewered past such mountainous passes as Despeñaperros and directed by angelic singing buskers, the cross of St James and groups of swarthy-faced youths: armpit relievers, wishing others good evenings, speculatively gesticulating as phantoms and spectres of the past, reconquistas: plying a trade of leather bags, selfie-sticks and iPad cases on blanket-topped pavements outside legitimised neon-lit trades and densities of claustrophobic promenades that, with turns, burst into spaces such as the triangulated Square of the Angels, and swept, towards bronze sculptors and immutable oscillations of human stationary statues, that in, mimicry of stasis, and smarter than hunger, stood around in amongst passageways with circumvolution and biased angles, that, furthered them along with incredulity leading them to cross the Plaza de Jacinto Benavente, which was partly curtain-sheeted at one end with blue, dust-retaining, building membranes that covered a particular attraction's alabaster crumble and then westward down Calle de la Bolsa to sibilant plosives from a Latinate vowel and bowel-emptied hungering to re-arranged menus, expressed, not so easily, in the absence of supposed superior English patronage but required by. Thus, they by-passed in voted elections, these inexplicable, unnamed and small concerns into others. Where, from every stone-grey shop, surrounded with porticoes and topped by wrought iron balconies, youthful Madrileños spied with heady Rioja, or some such, a warming warmth's warmingness in that night air with their most careful observance and practises and rituals. Ultimately, they went toward the Bourbon home of the restaurant ring-side seated steaks of bull fighting: the vast grand squared indices of the Herrera of the Plaza Mayor, a fusing of the sternest elements of the Renaissance and a dismissal of the dismal Baroque paused at and table-waited with calamaris and cat-called carambras.

"¡ Hola, Hola Inglés 'ere. Hola !"

That seemed perfect.

 So upon plastic chairs they sat. Poking their knees under the grease-wiped cloth which was decorated, spread with: cutlery, cruets, oils and sauces; runner-topped with tissue-thin layout paper, retained with draughtsman's clips and balanced upon uneven cobbles with utilised folded cardboard; proportionally placed, asymmetrically under, two foreshortened legs. Each separated stone in the quadrangle was fixed to its neighbour with in-fills of cement, identifiable as being unique but seen as similar: a whole courtyard conjoined in an archipelago: millions of stones, tramped upon by archival millions of the very richest of European passers-by, canonised by the very ground that Saint Isidro walked upon: he who offered a prayer and asked the well there to raise its waters well and deliver his drowning son from its depths and torturous chambers. And such passers-by were our four disciplines that too had been ritualistically netted by white-smocked waiters that fished upon the multitude's waverers.

So, in that fly-by-night tourist-catching trap they sat, studying and inspecting the laminated menu. Which, in broken languages of French, German and English invited them to swallow a perfect meal; everything upon it seemed to have a certain apple pie order. There were two types of menus: children-rated and adult-rated. The adult one obviously contained spirits, wines and beers. The other was similar in content but smaller in portion and price. Amalia looked at that one with an especial interest and thought about the future for her bambino-to-be. Its copious circumstantiated descriptions made her feel a little uneasy, what with the disjointing levels of corticotrophin-releasing hormone and human chorionic gonadotropin. She was somewhat disenchanted with the food that was enchantingly described. Arthur, unfettered as always would be first to choose, arbitrarily and unwisely, with fat pointing fingers and voluminous gestures that assumed the waiter was not conversant at all with his lingo.

"When in Rome," he imperiously announced, stabbing at the Paella.

For on their sides the others discovered, under an identifiable Union Flag, deliciously described delectations: Mexico: Chorizo, potato and cheese quesadilla (F: tortilla à la tarine de blé avec de la pomme de terre, du chorizo de porc et du fromage, et une sauce pimentée à la tomate et au piment); Italian: Roasted vegetable lasagne (NL:

Italiaanse pasta met spinazie, met geroosterde groenten in tomatensaus, met bechamelsaus en mozzarella); Spanish: Chargrilled Chicken and King Prawn Paelle (E: Pollo ahumado a la brasa con chorizo picante y pimientos rojos, paella con langostinos suculentos.). They each chose deleteriously and the waiter, Signor Ali Spagnola, noted thus and beetled away.

"Madrid is a mountain city and has a mountain's climate: three months of winter and nine months of hell. How quickly the temperature can change here," thought Jackie, who in her meteorological discernments of the cold had considered snuggling up to her pyrexic, over-bulked-up husband but thought, post pugilist marital discord, better of it and had therefore resided to looking furtively around, in glimpses, whilst he pontificated with a fustian explosion of bombast: "The square's blood-red rectilinearly balconies, within the tyranny of the orthogonal, squared, the central feature of Phillip the Third, King of the Spains: mounted in the middle with pride and with honour but remembered as insignificant and within this cyclic-quad square, that belied the horror of thousands of slaughtered bulls: auto-de-fé of the apostates: papal bulls in corrida and executions: the many that had died under his name, he rode. As you will note, it is harmoniously supported at its perimeter by golden-ratio'ed arches in deference to, and exemplified by, austere, authoritarian architecture. Its novenary entrances, unevenly spaced in corners and longer lines, permitted ingress to millions of tourists in summer and winters, mere footnotes within histories' circulations, those that expelled the Moriscos and their cheap labour, exploited in the harvest of the rice in rich man-made-mad Valencian fields. Plagued and blood-lusted, declined, and with the Dutch outside piously at the end, watching the four corners, is where we have come to, for we are at four corners as well, are we not."

Attis sat at a short length with Amalia close by. Arthur, pleased with his explanations, sat at the other short length with a carafe of ordinary house claret between himself and Jackie. Jackie sat obliviously alone, cold. Living through with what she had just learnt.

Behind the scenes, in the hidden kitchen, cardboard wrappers were removed and plastic films were pierced. Everything was piped hot within four minutes, stirred several times, rested and plated up with touching garnishees of lemon wedges or parsley where required. Preparatory to this coming to the customers a small earthenware bowl of off aioli and chili-infused, putrefied olives accompanied by two blown, amphora-styled, fatty jugs of tepid water were briskly whisked out by Signor Spagnola in a sophisticated way.

So whilst that craven trio dined upon the exotic fair, one member, Amalia, regally rejoicing in her motherhood, confined herself to stripping the fleshy husks off of queen olives and, with a blessing, nibbled discriminatingly from a packet of blanched almonds that, she, in her fruitful state hankered for and carried about her general silkened, appliqued personage.

Softly-spoken Attis announced, "This food is to die for. How is yours Arthur?"

42

"Shit," he replied pouring the remaining third of the wine into his fat, glass goblet. "I'd rather have good food than no food."

"I'm so clemmed. I could reet guzzle a scabby horse," brogued his northern wife.

"We are," he replied and, "you is," he thought without any equine equanimity, just nastily and maliciously.

A group of teenagers, who had been gathering under the balls of Phillip the Third's horse, moved off. Some of the youthful Spanish men were posturing with cojones and bravado. Their virility spoke of something. Off to get stoned and have fun, as requested, doubtless.

A nearby table, within earshot, contained a family of fat-butted Italian-Americans, fresh out of The Bronx. They were crossly-questioning Senor Spagnola with, "ifs" and "ands." Their demonstrative requests were rebounding off the square's grey slated, steep roofs, pinnacles and spires. They were that loud.

"Steak. I wanna steak. A big T-bone. Right here buddy."

Exasperated, the waiter turned away. He felt like offering his own water, wondering if that solution would calm them, or dilute their irritation somehow. For such a piece was not on his menu. Arthur seconding Attis' proposal, beckoned to him and ordered a Muscatel dessert wine and a crème brûlée, for the missus. At least Senor Spagnola could provide that to the more genteel folk.

Arthur then hawked up a frog spawn's worth of phlegm and snotted it backwards down his throat. He lit a post-dinner cigarette and puffed it surreptitiously upon the wind to his wife's frosty face.

"Got one of your faves there swan neck."

Amalia also requested a drink. But by this time slow steady rhythms of hormonal nausea came wobbling through her. The hustle bustle of tourists' faces staring at her, the stench of the over-greased food, the cigarettes all contributed in their way to that. She proceeded to: in this order: order: receive: sip from a large over-hot, gritted and granulated slew of murk that considered itself, with some arrogance, to be decaffeinated coffee. Its acidic, vile integument discoursed itself and trachealled into her stomach. In the reversed process of an un-welcomed orale, it became a colonic oral irrigation that in its dysentery and disaffection, unhealthily, with indigestive recitative and with a sharp belch, regurgitated a vomitus, staining slurry all down the front of her silken-white, operatic taffeta dress.

She wiped her gasping and horrified mouth with a paper napkin.

On reflection, it would have been for the best if she had ordered a soft drink instead.

"Jesus. Jesus. Jesus. What a disgrace I am." She said with much contempt.

Arthur, oblivious, kept drinking and smoking. Jackie kept looking around, anywhere but at him. Attis stood up to assist his partner, who exclaimed that she would need to return to the hotel. Obviously in her frowzed and doused, saturated state the embarrassment would be too much to remain. Already the Americans

44

were beginning to guffaw. She left wherewith. Attis apologised to the other couple and followed her.

"Great. So I will have to pay for this shite, always me. Funny that. O well. Jackie? Hello? Hello Jackie?"

Enforced to look she replied, "O it is no big deal, godspennys, thirty Euros at most. Someone has to cough owt. 'Ear all, see all, say nowt. Eat all, sup all, and pay nowt. And if ever tha does owt fer nowt allus do it fer thisen. But I am sure Attis will understand this and pay next time, tha knows."

The last spoons of the custard were swallowed. The last drops of the wine were drained. The last cigarette was stubbed. The bill was paid, eventually. Mr and Mrs Mackintosh stood up and moved off with the squabbling American family hissing from their cat's cradle of un-civilisation, massed in little junkets in this venerated world which they thought they could buy.

"I don't understand why you couldn't do a steak? Everywhere does steak. It is bullshit man, just bullshit. This pizza won't fill a gnat."

"Carlo, don't cuss, you should think of your body hun," hypocritically interjected the fat American's double-fatted wife, whose spaghetti strapped crop top was salami slicing deeply into her own fleshy hams of stuffed up shoulders. The gut of her double-tyre pneumatically bulged underneath and rested upon her rubbery thighs, like a second bosom, like an un-milked cow's distended udder.

She wobbled as she bellowed at her chocolate-smothered son, "Mind you don't eat too many of those Nun's Sighs or Ratón Pérez will come and get ya." And then looked back at her husband, "You know Carlo, maybe we should all work out when we get back home."

"Fitness! Bullshit, Jacobella! I could fit this whole pizza into my mouth. In one fucking go. It's gnats."

"Carlo!"

"Arribaderci," Arthur muttered silently to them.

Jackie and Arthur returned via the Plaza de Jacinto Benavente whereupon Arthur halted her with a touch of her elbow.

"Sorry."

"Aye, me too. I'm sorry I got cob on. It's just sometimes thee can be such a gawby, you really can. You should see yourself sometimes you big mardy wazzock."

"C'mon let's leave have a quick night cap. We are here on holiday. I do love you Jaxs."

"You barmpot."

Arthur gesticulated towards a covered cafe, full of personal remorse, conscious that his wife was feeling the cold and that that area had external heaters suspended within parasols, uneasily balanced on that square's footing, it would seem to do. They both concurred this silently and moreover it was almost ideally placed for one of their favourite pastimes, people watching: the injudicious modal of judgement upon other members of their shared humanity: considerations of the following: dress sense, gait, figure, fate, too. Invariably, imaginary tales of the stranger's lives were made up: all Mr Pootered and postulated as to how they may or may not be. Who could tell and who could they say? Arthur rolled his indelicate eyes around outlines of ladies' breasts, bottoms and legs, where apparent. Jackie juxtaposed herself into the arms of Hugh Grant and Edward Fox look-a-like Englishmen and romantic adventures. Both of them were less lying in subtle deceptions of no consequence and both of them were studying in three dimensional precision, movements that Muybridge tried to mechanical classify. A whole series of frozen frames that in a perpetual way rolled onwards imbibed with the principals that other people are inherently interesting, more than oneself, more often than not, so seen: hence the popularity of social media.

So the storm had passed in that heat-lazed day. Now they sat back in that late evening's cool, somnolent chairs and bathed in atmospheres and exotic imagery of fashions, styles: habitués and attitudes of passing strangers: Latinate matters, which they were in amongst, like prehistoric flies in golden amber but conversely equally outside of the empirical recording men of science. Two human mannequins still stood suited in Charlie Chaplain bowlers, boots and canes. Gauged by the small amount of money on their cardboard 'Gracias' mats, trade was not good that day. They too were phantasmagorically calcified. Both Mr and Mrs Mackintosh wondered how long they had been there, although they did not convey this question to each other.

Svelte Jackie, ever conscious of her figure, ordered just one Cornetto, a strawberry one. She un-peeled its conical wrapper and began slurping its pleasant sweetness. Arthur ordered a large gin.

Atoning for his earlier mistake, one which the desire for an earlier gin had precipitated, he raised the glass into the air with a quick saludo: "Viva España !"

Presently, an accordion player wandered through the collection of warmed tables and chairs. He was viewed by the cafe's patrons with discordant snarls and finger flicking observations. Even the owners of the cafe observed him in much the same way. For it seemed he returned to their cafe with regularity, like a wasp does to ice-cream vendors. However, it must be said, whilst his begging presence was unwarranted, his musicianship was delightful and unparalleled. Initially, the Parisian timbre of the accordion seemed out of place in Madrid but not so if one conceived its true cosmopolitan and international flavour. He staved his way towards Arthur and Jackie because, and only because, they had both smiled at him and he therefore perceived that there may be a chance for his work to be rewarded. The cheerful melody of 'Melancolie' swirled around them. It back-dropped their improved atmosphere and cordialité. Jackie removed a glass amphora from her bag, which was in the way of her purse, and tipped him a five euro "Si" minor note. He noted it, bowed, smiled back and moved off. His music's sweet pretty melody wafted away.

Mileva Anastasiadou

Mileva Anastasiadou is a neurologist, living and working in Athens, Greece. Her work can be found in Ofi press magazine, Infective Ink, the Molotov Cocktail, Foliate Oak, HFC journal, Down in the Dirt, Minus paper, Massacre, Pendora, Maudlin house, Menacing Hedge, Scarlet Leaf Review, Nebula Rift, and soon in Midnight Circus, AntipodeanSF, Big Echo:Critical SF, Blood and Thunder:Musings on the Art of Medicine, Jellyfish Review, and the Fear of Monkeys.

Follow her on Facebook: https://www.facebook.com/milevaanastasiadou/

The 12 Hits of Christmas

On the first hit of Christmas

The crisis had hit his door before, but he had refused to open it. Or better, somebody had knocked on the door, but it must have been the wind, not the crisis, for back then, whoever tried to enter, did not insist. It could have been the postman after all. This time though, it was something stronger, that hit once, twice, and then broke open the door, which could no longer resist the inflicted force.

There came a slight discomfort, as the door was becoming larger and larger and he could not close it, which little by little transformed into panic, with all its accompanying characteristics: fast heart rate, dizziness, numbness of the limbs, along with the sensation that the air was not enough. He took some deep breaths, as if the amount of oxygen in the room would grow, if he tried harder.

"Like when you puff harder to keep the cigarette lit," he thought in panic, but the metaphor did not calm him down. Nor did his thoughts who ran unrestrained on his financial problems. On the contrary, the more he asphyxiated, the greedier he became for air. He recalled a show he had watched years ago on tv, and ran to the kitchen. He emptied a plastic bag, and stuck it to his face.

"I wonder how on earth there was so much air in an empty bag," he wondered, when he started regaining his composure.

"Did I almost die?" he wondered, staring at the blinking lights of the Christmas tree at the apartment across the street. He had not realized that Christmas was coming, until this happened. And this was just the first blow. And it was a heavy blow indeed.

On the second hit of Christmas

He smoked a couple of joints, while thinking about it; he should visit a doctor.

Instead of calling a specialist though, he called his best friend.

"You'd better have a good reason for calling me this early, Glue".

Glue was his nickname. He earned it years ago, when he used to sniff glue, paint thinners, gasoline, or whatever was at hand. It came naturally, paraphrasing his real name, which was Lou. He had given up on all this crap though, since he no longer needed any of it. He already had the means to ensure better fixes for himself, without having to compromise with cheap alternatives.

"For heaven's sake Mike, it's 5 o'clock in the afternoon! It is not early, not even for me. Come over here fast".

Mike was there five hours later.

On the upper shelf of the closet, in which Lou rarely entered, except in the case of emergency, since he could barely stand the chaos in it, let alone deal with it, a bell and an angel had taken refuge. Old and forgotten Christmas ornaments from Lou's family house, they once anticipated the festive season, in order to be hung on the family Christmas tree, so as to fulfill the meaning of their existence. Many years have passed, since they last decorated some tree branches, as Lou was not that fond of Christmas.

"Poor guy! I cannot even begin to imagine what is in store for him," said Bell.

"You really feel sorry for him, after all he's done to us?" asked Angel, anger all over his face.

"I've known him since he was a kid, I cannot help it".

Silence prevailed in the closet again, interrupted by the ringing of the phone, which was louder than other times, as it managed to wake Lou up. In the back of his mind, he felt that he had forgotten to do something of great importance. Then it hit him. He had to go to work. Considering the expenses and the loans, he could not afford to lose this job.

"Mike, get the phone. I must get dressed. I have to get to work," he shouted at his best friend, who was still sleeping on the sofa. Mike searched on the floor blindly, in order to trace where this annoying noise was coming from.

"Who was it?" asked Lou, entering the living room, all dressed up for work.

"You don't have to run after all," said Mike.

"Will you get serious and tell me who it was on the phone?" asked Lou, taking a last look in the mirror, arranging his hair.

"I'm telling you. You don't have a job to run to. You just got fired".

The air began to get thicker and thicker again. That was a heavy hit indeed, wasn't it Lou? Are you strong enough to handle it?

On the third hit of Christmas

Lou was standing out of the doctor's office, waiting for his turn.

"It is obviously an attack," announced the doctor.

"Like an alien attack or something, doc?"

"A panic attack," he explained, after throwing a contemptuous glance at Lou.

Lou avoided any further questions, as he watched the doctor write and then hand him a prescription.

"You will come back in a month," the doctor said strictly, as if it was Lou's mistake that he suffered from those panic attacks.

On leaving the building, he took a glance of the wall across the street.

$$D+L=\heartsuit$$

Never before had he felt touched by such manifestations of affection and tenderness. This time though, a bell rang in his mind. He almost heard it literally. And he felt that well known dizziness, which meant that the air would not seem enough in a little while.

"These panic attacks, the doctor was talking about, are getting way too frequent," he thought, while running to the closest drugstore to get his medicines.

On the fourth hit of Christmas

The lights abruptly went out, and Lou had to blindly search for the key to the closet, in search of his lost flashlight.

"What next?" he wondered, as he searched around with one hand, while trying to keep the lighter lit with the other. The answer came naturally, when after a while, a little silver bell landed on his head and then, after multiple rebounds on random places, eventually reached the floor.

"How did these stupid little ornaments get here? I am certain I had put them away in a box years ago".

"Are you calling us stupid?" said Angel, not being able to stand the insult. It is one thing to be kept locked and forgotten in a closet, but it is completely outrageous when your patience and your sacrifices are not even appreciated.

Lou looked around puzzled.

"I must be going crazy. Or is it the side effects of the drugs? Or maybe the pizza I ate last night?" he thought loudly.

"Sure, blame it on the pizza now".

"Well, I have to confess, that we caused all this," said Angel after a silent pause. "You have forgotten us in this closet for so long, that we had to do something to get out of here".

"We did it for your own good as well," added Bell reluctantly. "Well, we mean no harm, but you know... You have abandoned us here in the closet for so long, that we felt obliged to report you".

"Report me?"

"It is not neither personal, nor that important," said Angel, spinning around Lou's head. "We reported your lack of decorations for the past ten years, and now the procedures have started".

"Procedures?" Lou took comfort in repeating the words of his company, in the form of questions.

"Nothing unusual, just the twelve hits of Christmas," said Bell, in the most reassuring tone.

The lights were on again, and Lou grabbed the flashlight and ran out of the closet and into the streets, still in his pajamas.

On the fifth hit of Christmas

Next morning, he woke up at Mike's place. Strangely, Mike was already awake.

"Panic attacks, that's what the doctor said".

"Is it serious?"

"He did not tell me. He gave me some medicines though".

"Hey, I got a neighbor who's a dentist. Let's go ask".

"He's a dentist, Mike. How on earth should he know?"

"Come on. He surely knows more than we do".

"So, you have panic attacks? That means you know very well what it's all about. It's what I get when I wait for a patient, and a miserable neighbor comes instead, with an even more miserable friend, to ask me what happens when I wait for a patient, and a miserable neighbor comes instead, with an even more miserable friend... and so on. You get it, right? That's a panic attack".

The two visitors stepped back slowly, as the doctor threw a lighter towards their direction, which barely hit Lou's arm.

That was hardly a hit. I bet you can handle more Lou.

On the sixth hit of Christmas

Lou is sitting on a bench. There, in the middle of the playground, stands a tree, decorated with small colorful balls, bells, and little angels. Surprisingly, he throws a glance towards the tree in sympathy. If the bells and the angels had consciousness, although they certainly have not, as Lou has to remind himself, they would only want to accomplish their purpose in life.

Lou is wondering if he, too, has a purpose in life

"My purpose is certainly not as clear as the purpose of a chair, a table, or even a little bell," he thinks moments before he closes his eyes. And just when he gets lost in thought on the meaning of his own existence...

BANG

A ball hits him on the head.

The little angel of the closet is spinning around his head again.

You are fine, Lou. Let us see know how much more you can handle.

On the seventh hit of Christmas

Lou was not certain as to whether he could count the hit by the ball or not. A stray soccer ball that popped onto his head while he was almost asleep, could be considered a coincidence after all.

The phone, which kept ringing, interrupted his daydreaming.

"I am calling from the hospital. A young man has been transferred here in a coma. You are the only person he has talked to, during the last twenty four hours. Could you possibly come over for some further clarifications?"

Lou stood frozen for a while.

"So this was the lesson I was supposed to learn? The ball on my head... everything... They all mean that life could end just as abruptly as it began? By a stupid ball, or an overdose? Is that the lesson?"

As he looked around, he noticed the wall across the street. The graffiti drew his attention for a moment.

D+L=♥

"What kind of answer is this? A stupid graffiti on a wall that does not make any sense," he thought to himself.

"If this is the lesson, then I don't want to learn," he

screamed out of the open window and then turned to the taxi driver's direction, who had been looking at him, worried, through the mirror.

"Don't mind me. Please, be as fast as you can".

On the eighth hit of Christmas

Mike is fine. Lou's house though, is not fine at all. At first, Lou thought it was hit by robbers. Beer cans were thrown all over the place, half-empty bottles of wine on the table, full ashtrays. Strangely enough, nothing is missing. It seems as if somebody came, threw a party, and then forgot to turn off the music.

"In case you wonder you forgot to lock the closet," said Angel. "There may have been a miracle that made us talk, fly, drink and dance, but we still are incapable of breaking locks. Well, those up above, they say you have not understood anything yet. You do seem to have a very good time, though. I think that all this nonsense they have been teaching us up there, are all useless. Dear Bell, will you pass me the joint please?"

"We are only experimenting." Bell tried to justify herself.

"Interesting experiment I would add. Who cares about getting hung on a Christmas tree, as long as there's wine?" Bell and Angel burst into loud laughter.

"You only exist because I keep you alive in my sick mind," Lou cried angrily.

"Right. Are you interested in the latest gossip?" asked Bell playfully, as if it was the most normal thing in the world for Lou to be interested in gossip, especially when coming from two Christmas ornaments.

"I am not interested at all," he said, and looked to the ceiling, as if he was talking to a mysterious invisible creature.

"I don't care what you think of me, up there. I never believed in Christmas, or in Santa Claus, or even in God. In fact, I would rather you didn't exist. Because, if it is all true, you are then responsible for all the misery of the world".

"Nice speech, mate, but you got it all wrong. You will figure it out. You just need time," said Angel after a long pause that seemed to last for ages.

On the ninth hit of Christmas

The idea got wedged as a bullet in his brain, so different and bright than anything he had ever thought of, and powerful enough to disable any other sense, so that his whole existence merged into a new-found happiness, which was completely different to any artificial paradise he had visited before.

After unboxing all the Christmas ornaments and placing the long forgotten Christmas tree into the living room, he called the only person he thought of, whom he could share his joy with.

"Whatever happened to you?" asked Mike on the other side of the line, who had just got out of the hospital.

"We should change our perspective, Mike. All signs show to a different direction. All that happened to us show us the way...".

"What way?"

"The way to become better persons," said Lou in a determined voice.

"Can you please become a better person by yourself? I don't feel well enough to make important decisions at the moment," Mike told him before he abruptly hung up the phone. Lou had no money, no job, not any available friends, but just before midnight, he managed to decorate the most beautiful Christmas tree.

On the tenth hit of Christmas

Two blocks away, near the mall, Santa wanders in the city. Truth is that in the old times, his work was limited to supervising the construction of the toys. Things have changed lately. The crisis has affected not only the known world, but also the less known one, the one that some people even consider unreal. The worst of all is that the apathy of people to all that is happening to them fueled those up above with ideas, so they now insist on tight budgets, fiscal adjustments, and work intensification, without reason after all, as up above, they do not use money at all.

Santa had to look for a job. Who would hire him though? You cannot work as Santa, if you are not dressed as Santa, even if you are Santa. Never had he suspected that clothes could cause him such a big problem, or that the clothes would be more reliable than a saint himself.

"I am a dead man," he thought to himself, sinking in despair, while thinking about the recent gossip. Donner and Rudolph fell in love, and decided to run away. They have sprayed their love all over the town, on every wall they found empty. Only angels and spirits undertook those cases in the past, but due to the recent cuts, the two reindeer had to take care of Lou too, this year. Rumors say that they were assigned this case only because "Lou" is also the nickname of Rudolph.

It did not go as planned though. After they discovered they were soul mates, they only pretended to work on Lou's case, and decided to escape and drink all day, as the research they had conducted on Lou had proved extremely pleasant.

Santa's eyes shone when he saw Lou crossing the street. And then came the idea. Santa grabbed Lou by the neck and threw him down. Lou did not have any time to react properly or defend himself.

"Stop," yelled a girl from afar.

"Sorry mate, this had to be done," Santa whispered in Lou's ear and ran away in joy, hoping the two reindeer would give up on their plans, now that they would have to get a bit more engaged in Lou's case.

On the eleventh hit of Christmas

"For the next few days, you should be very careful," the doctors told him.

"Do you want me to call somebody to come and get you?" asked the girl beside him, the same girl that saved him from the aspiring villain that had attacked him earlier.

"I'll make it on my own," he said taking a look at the girl for the first time.

"That's out of the question. You heard what the doctors just said".

He thanked her politely and headed for the exit.

"I can't leave you alone," she insisted. "Besides, we haven't even introduced ourselves. I am Dorothy," she said offering her hand for a handshake.

They decided to go to the terrace, above Lou's house, in order to watch the sunrise. It would not be any sunrise. Christmas was dawning in just a few hours.

"If this was a dream, how would you call it? A pleasant one or a nightmare?" Dorothy asked him.

"It becomes better and better by the minute," answered Lou, who could not believe the words he was saying. Not because they were not true, but because they were. He felt something he could not yet define. Perhaps something like hope.

Lou started to suspect that this could be another hit. He had to confess though, it was much more pleasant than the previous ones.

On the twelfth hit of Christmas

Just before the Christmas bells rang, the sky ahead of them, began to change colors, yet instead of acquiring the usual golden color of the dawn, it was getting darker and darker, until it got purple and then a wild wind started to rise, that almost took them away.

Lou and Dorothy could not keep their eyes open any longer, but they still held hands tightly. It took them a while to realize that nothing stable was beneath their feet any more, that they were not on the terrace, that nothing familiar was around.

They were flying. Before they even had the chance to enjoy the trip, the wind began to calm, and it was as if a magical hand placed them gently on the ground.

Two reindeer appeared in front of them, not just any two reindeer, but two reindeer that could talk too. Nothing could surprise Lou any more, unlike Dorothy who stood beside him open mouthed.

"I am Lou and this is Donner," the reindeer introduced themselves.

"They must be Santa's reindeer" said Dorothy in low voice and Lou nodded.

"Well, actually Lou is my nickname, my real name is Rudolph. You must have heard all the rumors about us, haven't you?"

They had not heard a thing. Lou remembered the graffiti on the walls. He then recalled the gossip, which the little bell had mentioned, and regretted his decision to ignore her words.

"How weird! We did our best so that those rumors could reach you ears. We are supposed to be in love and determined to not work for Santa any more".

"But... this is impossible," Dorothy muttered through her teeth. "I mean you could be in love of course, but not working for Santa should be out of the question".

"You are absolutely right," said Donner. "It is rather impossible indeed, yet even Santa believed it and hit you, in order to make us focus on our work".

"But," Lou presented his objections, "whoever hit me,

64

did not look like Santa at all".

"He certainly was Santa, who knew we were on you case".

"So you were on my case," mumbled Lou.

"Our goal though was even higher than the usual stuff. We did not only want to make you love Christmas".

Lou thought that he and Dorothy had the same initials as the reindeer. D+L. Donner and Lou. Dorothy and Lou (the human).

"So long, twelve hits of Christmas. The time has come now for the twelve days of Christmas!" shouted Donner in ecstasy, as the Christmas bells began ringing from somewhere faraway, and the landscape was becoming blurry little by little, until it became all bright and gold.

Back on the terrace, they looked at each other as if they could not believe what had just happened to them, yet they recognized in each other's eyes the same magical experience, without speaking a word.

The Christmas bells were still ringing, and Lou knew; that was certainly the final hit.

Barry Parham

Barry Parham is the award-winning author of humor columns, essays and short stories. He is a recovering software freelancer and a music fanatic.

Parham is the author of the 2009 sleeper, "Why I Hate Straws," his debut collection of humor and satire including the prize-winning stories, 'Going Green, Seeing Red' & 'Driving Miss Conception.'

In October 2010, Parham published "Sorry, We Can't Use Funny," another award-winning collection of general-topic satire and humor, and the more targeted "Blush: Politics and other unnatural acts." He followed up in 2011 with "The Middle-Age of Aquarius," a growing-old-but-not-so-gracefully vehicle for the award-winners 'Comfortably Dumb,' 'Snowblind' and 'The Zodiac Buzz-Killer.'

"Full Frontal Stupidity" (2012), Parham's 5th collection of humor, satire and observations, features more award-winning stories, including 'Skirts vs. Skins' and 'Scenes From a Maul.' He followed up the next year with a brace of collections, "Chariots of Ire" and "You Gonna Finish That Dragon?" and most recently published his 8th compilation, "Maybe It's Just Me."

Parham's work has also been featured in three national humor anthologies:
"My Funny Valentine" (2011)
"Open Doors: Fractured Fairy Tales" (2012)
"My Funny Major Medical" (2012)

Equally Cold Calls

(Sometimes you have to bite the dog back.)

Ever get an unsolicited telemarketing call and decide to just run with it? You should. It's free, it's good for you, and it has zero trans-fat.

Besides, toying with telemarketers is one of your guaranteed Constitutional rights, enumerated right there between your right to have a seizure and your right to not have your bare arms searched.

And ... they asked for it. After all:

- *they* called *you*
- it's legal for telemarketers to lie to *you*, so lying to *them* is pretty much open season
- technically speaking, telemarketers aren't from this planet

To be fair, it's (usually) not the telemarketers' fault, especially that last point about being aliens. Telemarketing is just a job like any other job, except for the part where everybody you speak to hates you. Cold-calling people all day every day is a hard life. I know. I've done it.

In the mid-80s, as part of my post-university career plan – my plan was to retire *first*, then maybe settle into a career later, what's the big rush -- I packed my six personal possessions (two shirts, two pairs of jeans, a pair of shoes and a music player) and moved from Southern California to North Miami.

When I arrived in South Florida, however, I discovered that Miami had officially defected to Cuba, and no bar or lounge in the land would hire a bartender who didn't know how to *habla*.

I had to find a job, and quickly. And since I wasn't qualified for your normal South Florida entry-level jobs — I didn't have the seed money to invest in a starter bale of marijuana, and I didn't know how to say, in Spanish, "Hi, my name's Barry and I'm available to be your international cocaine mule" — I took a job as a telemarketer.

Five days a week, we would huddle in oddly-stained cubes with mountains of thermal-printed lists inside windowless rooms that always smelled of pork and plantains, and for hour after hour we would cold-call car dealerships with names like Tulsa Dodge World (*"Home of the Steel Wheel Real Deal!"*) and Big Tiny's One-Owner Used-Auto Graveyard. (*"Where High Prices Go To Die!"*)

And our plum job was to sell radio ads to these caffeine-crazed, margin-guarding, bolo-tie-wearing deal-dancers.

It was a mad, maddening, Gatling-gun-paced whipsaw of a ride that drove me so insane I ended up getting engaged. But let's not pick at *that* thread. Not today.

Needless to say, I didn't stick around long enough to sweat and claw my way to a leadership position in the coveted inner circle of North Miami Nondescript Strip Mall-Based

Outbound Call Center Boiler Room middle management. Oh, el *heck*, no.

So now I'm just a simple single guy who got a cold call, and decided to run with it.

And when I say "run with it," I don't just mean simply re-running one of the anti-cold-call classics, like pretending you only speak a foreign language, or asking them to hold for a second while you put the phone on the counter, lock your house, go have your car detailed, catch a movie, get that nose job you've been putting off, and then drive to the grocers with your full monthly shopping list.

I'm talking about a full-on, fangs-drawn but still low-key hostility. I'm talking about a focused, dedicated, short-term confrontational relationship, one that demands equal doses of spicy subtlety, rich, lightning-fast ripostes, and a dash of hob-nailed boots.

And it's not often I make a commitment.

[*ring*]

Me: This is Barry.

Leaf-Slayer: Hi. This is Mumbled Name calling from Leaf-Slayer. Is this James Parham?

Me: Yes.

Leaf-Slayer: Here at Leaf-Slayer, our motto is "We H8 Leaves!" Isn't that clever!

Me: Yes, you should all be very proud.

Leaf-Slayer: See how we spelled *hate* with an "8" there?

Me: Lady, this is a *phone call*. I can't see how you spelled "hate."

Leaf-Slayer: What?

Me: Good word, though, "hate." I'm contempl8ting it this very minute.

Leaf-Slayer: Is this James Parham?

Me: Yes, still. What was your name again?

Leaf-Slayer: Mumbled Name.

Me: Hi, Missus Name. Or can I call you Mumbled?

Leaf-Slayer: We've been trying to reach you about an estimate.

Me: No, thank you.

Leaf-Slayer: Is this James Parham?

Me: Yes, darling. It *is* "darling," isn't it?

Leaf-Slayer: We've been trying to reach you about an estimate.

Me: I know how you feel. I've been trying to ignore you trying to reach me about an estimate.

Leaf-Slayer: Is this James?

Me: Yes, you persistent, hot thing. It's still me. Hey, I'm gonna go out on a limb here and ask: you called for a reason?

Leaf-Slayer: We've been trying to reach you about an estimate.

Me: No, thank you. Good-bye.

Leaf-Slayer: You've picked another solution?

Me: No. Good-bye.

Leaf-Slayer: What?

Me: Good-bye. "Good-bye." It's a fairly common word except, apparently, in telemarketing circles, and other primitive cultures. Look it up.

Leaf-Slayer: What?

Me: Sorry. Google it.

Leaf-Slayer: You've picked another solution?

Me: No.

Leaf-Slayer: What?

Me: What are you wearing?

Leaf-Slayer: Is this James?

Me: Hold on, I'll check my camp underwear.

Leaf-Slayer: What?

Me: Yes, it's me. Assuming I can read my Mom's handwriting.

Leaf-Slayer: What?

Me: Look, I don't need my foliage slain.

Leaf-Slayer: I understand your hesitation. What are you using now for vital, life-enhancing gutter management?

Me: It's complicated.

Leaf-Slayer: What?

Me: From August till November, I sit on my roof and slap leaves out of my gutters with a jaded ferret who read too much Sylvia Plath. Unless, of course, it's a day when my Druid cult is meeting.

Leaf-Slayer: Is this James?

Me: No, is this?

Leaf-Slayer: What?

Hema Nataraju

Hema used to be a Human Resources professional in another life, but these days, she works full time for the toughest boss in the world - her 3-year old daughter. When she isn't looking, Hema drinks coffee and writes stories. Her goal is to invent a device to write down story ideas from her brain when she's putting her toddler to bed.

She is a word nerd who can speak seven languages, but cannot summon a word when she most needs it. She makes up for what she cannot say with her writing. Her work has been featured on The Huffington Post.

Hema lives in the San Francisco Bay Area with her husband and daughter and a mountain of laundry that she lovingly calls Padfoot.

She blogs here: http://www.hemas-mixedbag.com

Follow her on Twitter: @m_ixedbag https://twitter.com/m_ixedbag

Shave

Garth, the event coordinator was at the venue an hour before the meeting was to begin. He checked the AV setup one more time, straightened a few errant chairs and went over special meal requests, mentally checking them off as he went down the list. What's a special garlic meal? So peculiar! He fired up his laptop and the projector screen whirred. The SHAVE oath appeared in bold green font.

SHAVE always sounded zany to Garth, more like a hipster barber shop than what it really stood for - Society for Human and Vampire Empathy.

Garth and the other vampires were meeting human delegates face-to-face for the very first time.

The humans had wanted to talk about some life threatening emergency. Alfred, the president of the Vampire chapter of SHAVE had thought it best to discuss face-to-face. Their monthly Skype call wasn't going to cut it. The humans had said something about putting their lives on line for the betterment of their people and agreed to meet them.

What is with these humans playing the martyr? Vampires had lived in perfect harmony with humans for some time now. They bought blood only from certified blood banks for vampires, never jumped on anyone in the dead of the night (excuse the pun) and almost never complained about the declining quality of human blood these days.

Just last week, Fiona, Garth's girlfriend, had unknowingly drunk the blood of a guy who ate at Taco Bell every day. Poor girl had had nausea and gas for days. Tainted, unhealthy blood was the bane of their existence these days. *Must bring this up at the next meeting.*

But today, for once, dinner won't be just about eating. He expected arguments and fireworks. *We'll be having dinner with dinner today*! Garth chuckled internally at that thought. It would be fun to dissect this meeting with Fiona later over a chilled Bloody Mary and their favorite comedy - 'The Twilight Series'.

The vampires had been instructed to drink their fill before the meeting. As a gesture of respect, blood would not be served to vampires during the meeting. The humans walked in half an hour later than the appointed time with ashen faces and terrified eyes. Braids of garlic dangled around their warm slender necks. He forced himself to focus on something other than their soft fleshy necks.

"A warm welcome to our very first in-person meeting". Garth looked around with a smile, but nobody laughed. *Some sense of humor for dinner, anyone?*

"Ahem! Anyway, let's all rise and repeat the SHAVE oath"

While they recited distractedly, two petrified waiters came in bearing clattering dinner trays. The pungent odor of their special meals replaced the air in the room. Emboldened by their garlicky allies, Patrick the president of the Human Chapter began,

"Thank you for meeting us, We're here to talk about..."

Barney, the youngest vampire and the newest SHAVE member was getting a little carried away by the mesmerizing human scent. To calm himself, he discreetly brought out his hip flask and took a sip. A drop of blood somehow escaped his lips and drooled down to his chin.

Fear fogged Patrick's brain. He mumbled something inaudibly. The rest of the humans shuffled in their seats. The room grew hotter. Garth had an inexplicable urge to run his tongue over his fangs. Garth had now started a 'lick'. The other vampires joined in, unable to stop.

Hearts drumming in their heads, the humans stood up. Alfred was apologizing profusely between licks, but the nervous human huddle was heading for the door.

A thick sheet of darkness fell over the room. The powercut couldn't have come at a worse time.

The SHAVE meeting had now become a very hairy situation.

Brena Mercer

I eat and sleep in Tucson, Arizona. I have a Bachelors in
Literature from the University of California at Santa Barbara.
During the course of those studies, it was not uncommon to have
up to five books a week to read. Was Dorian Gray a vampire?
Why was he hanging out with a poodle in Gorky Park, and at the
same time he got a slave girl pregnant on a southern plantation?
My education is a blur, but I did teach Developmental English,
so I know all about commas.

"Stretch – the story of a dog's life" is a book of paintings and
text, and it is available at Blurb –
http://www.blurb.ca/b/2360307-stretch

"Bisbee and Madly Psychedelic Socks" is a satirical Chapbook
and a spoof on publishing. It is available on Amazon –
https://www.amazon.com/dp/1519280181

"Death and Dawn" is a humorous detective novel available on
Amazon – https://www.amazon.com/dp/B01JZZRYGS

Dirty, Dirty, Dirty Money

Who wipes their butt with a dollar bill? The only person
who may know is the doctor who treated the deviant for a
raging staph infection and inexplicable cocaine high. Was it a
protest against the financial institutions, dire necessity,
impaired judgment, or simple cruelty? The important question
is how did it end up in the gutter in front of my house? That will

remain a mystery, but for a penniless person a dollar found is proof of God, but this God has a mean streak. I watched the usual homeless people walk by. Each of them scurried over to the enticing green paper, bent down for a closer look, snapped upright, backed up slowly, and gave it a wide berth.

I live in a small town of rogues, miscreants, and people of oddness. There are approximately one thousand full time residents in the area called Old Bisbee. We could provide all the crewmembers for a cruise ship or fit into two Boeing 777s. There are more than four times that many people at every Celine Dion concert. Living in a town this small is like having all your Facebook friends for neighbors with no option to unfriend them.

The locals proudly and loudly claim to celebrate diversity. It is not much of a celebration as there isn't any. There are more homeless people than Blacks and Asians combined, and they formed a closed tribe many years ago. When new ones come to town and infringe on their begging rights, they run them off with sticks and knives. The only way to support the "diversity is a party" idea is to embrace the culture of the down-and-outers and act like their lifestyle is just not a big deal.

I live on Main Street and have a front row seat for the daily parade of familiar, colorful, and thought-provoking street people. They made a decision and put forth the effort required to live an outdoorsy life, and they wear it like an "I voted" lapel sticker.

Is it possible I am one misstep away from being one of them? I don't have any street survival skills. I would probably live in pajamas, put a donation box on the sidewalk, and recite The Rime of the Ancient Mariner. People would walk by and say, "She's harmless." I prefer my warm fuzzy life where I can spend my time pondering important information about 3D printers, face blindness, duct tape wallets, art from Cheetos, and tiny houses. These people remind me of how strange and startling life can be.

Who are these people? I feel like a code breaker when I hear them talk about their lives before they took up residence on the streets. The guy who went to Harvard actually hitch hiked through Boston. The one who was a bigwig at IBM simply found part of an antique IBM computer in a trash bin, and it looked important. The guy who claims to be a blue blood noticed his veins look blue through his skin. The man who swears he wrote "Sad-eyed Lady of the Lowlands" believes that because he appears to be the only one who knows all the words to that song. It is not easy to imagine their descent from grace, but I try.

Staple guy is always barefoot, and no one knows his name. He spends his days pulling staples out of power poles. The flyers have disappeared, but the staples remain. He is making the world a tidier, therefore better, place. I have never had a compulsive episode to rival his dedication and focus. Sometimes I picture him as a child crying himself to sleep after being spanked for getting mud on his clean clothes. He grew into a kind and considerate man. His last year of high school, he met a girl who didn't want to graduate with her virginity intact. The following summer they got married. She really didn't particularly like him. She was young and assumed her job was to make him into the man she wanted him to be. She really didn't know what kind of man she wanted, so she tortured him with the impossibility of pleasing her. He got a job cleaning rental cars after they were returned. One day a car came in that was completely trashed. Something in him snapped. He scrubbed that car until it sparkled, got behind the wheel, and sped away.

81

The car was found two weeks later in Bakersfield. He cleaned it up, dumped it, and kept on going.

Madame Marty is a cross-dressing pugilist with a laugh like a machine gun. He wears a black curly wig, flippy short skirts, and tight tank tops. He does all of this to incite drunks to beat him up. I gave him five dollars and broke my no conditions rule of charity. I insisted he was never to make eye contact with me again. When he sees me he quickly looks away, and I respect him for holding up his end of the bargain. I imagine Marty came from circus folks. His parents were underachievers in that world. His mother sold tickets, and his father cleaned up after the animals. His mother wanted a daughter, and his father lovingly beat him daily just for shits and grins. When Marty was twelve, his father ran off with a plate spinner. His mother hooked up with a person of dubious character in the next town. Marty tried to adjust but spent most of his time in juvenile hall. When he was fourteen he hit the road and begged his way to the southwest where it is warm enough to sleep outside.

Dumper (probably not his real name) spends all day walking from one end of town to the other. He carries cardboard signs. "Need money to buy food for my dog." "Need money to feed my baby." "Need money to buy tampons for my wife." We all know he doesn't have a dog, baby, or wife. We also know he will not work for food. He sleeps in the bushes, smells like a wild animal, and is easily provoked. I imagine he was born with a smirk on his face giving his mother the finger. I imagine his parents dropped him off at a truck stop and kept on going. I don't acknowledge him when I pass him on the street. He does not like to be ignored and calls me ugly names. There are probably several shallow graves in the desert and a warrant somewhere for his arrest.

Booger needs to wipe his nose. He is raising his daughter, Baby Spice, alone on the streets. As a responsible father he has provided an abandoned car for them to sleep in. (Someday she may write a kick-ass memoir.) She dresses like any five year old who wants to look like a hooker. I don't know where she goes when he is in jail for slashing tires or breaking windows. I imagine he came from a family with dark secrets. His father teaches at a university, makes paper dolls of his favorite students so he can pretend to undress them, and composes threatening chain letters. His mother teaches at a high school, starts vicious rumors about her colleagues, and encourages young girls to cut themselves. The mother of Booger's daughter died of an overdose soon after she was born. He thought he would get respect and attention from his parents, but they still think of him as a big fat zero. Now he is just passing time on the streets.

G.I. Joe darts around with a walkie-talkie pretending to shoot people with a stick. Tinky Winky wears hideous old lady polyester dresses and carries a pocketbook with his elbow bent. Bulldozer sleeps on the roof of the coffee shop, always wants twenty dollars for a drug fix, and gives everyone the stink eye. Squirrel got caught sleeping in a park restroom in a mummy suit out of toilet paper to keep warm. The tragedy of that is no one took a picture.

Somehow with all our differences, we all know poop on a dollar bill is just not right. Poop on a twenty may have been a different story. For me it would have to be a hundred dollar bill. I would have worn gloves and put it in a plastic bag. I would have handed the bag to a cashier in a store and had a different story to tell. After a week a storm came and washed the offending dollar away and with it proof of God.

Don Ake

Don Ake is a modern day "renaissance man". His "day job" consists of being a transportation industry expert at an economic research firm. In his spare time, he uses his tremendous sense of humor and sharp wit to write his Ake's Pains blog. The laugh-out -loud posts are so popular that he organized them into a book, Just Make Me A Sammich. He has an MBA from the University of Akron and resides with his wife in Northeast Ohio, very close to his hometown of Akron.

Buy his book! – http://donake.net/just-make-me-a-sammich-book
Check out his blog – http://akespains.blogspot.com

I Went Hunting in the Bushlands

Sometimes men have to do things they don't really want to do all for the benefit of their marriage. Okay, many times we must do these unpleasant things. All right, often it seems that marriage can be just one uncomfortable thing after another.

Recently, I did something for the first time in my life in an attempt to please my wife. I actually went to a nursery and landscaping store to buy some shrubbery for my wife's birthday. Now you must understand I am not a horticulturalist. I am probably a horti-counterculturalist. I am not interested at all in bushes or shrubs. I don't even notice them unless they grow so much they get in my way or they start to die. At which time I say astute things to my wife such as, "That shrub needs trimmed," or "That bush looks likes its dying; maybe you should do something."

So, why did I find myself anxiously looking over a large selection of greenery? Two years ago the township decided to clean the drainage ditch at the side of our yard for the first time in 19 years. They came out one day without warning and completed the task. They had the option of clearing all vegetation within five feet from the ditch to give their equipment proper clearance. Fortunately, to get to our ditch they could have gained access by clearing only about a foot of foliage. Unfortunately, they decided to take the whole five feet.

My wife had spent years getting that part of the yard just how she liked it. It was beautiful, even to a horti-counterculturalist like me. My wife was livid. She wanted to scream at our trustees. Of course, screaming wouldn't bring back the plants and such, so I offered to pay for professional landscapers to redo the area next year.

But my wife didn't take the deal. Probably a combination of principle (Why should we pay for someone else's stupid behavior) and personal feelings (This is my yard and I will deal with it.) However, what was left of the bushes and shrubs after the township massacre started to regenerate. Just like when we suffer a setback in life and think the situation will be horrible forever, it does get better over time. In this case, the bank actually started to fill in wonderfully. It looked great except for two noticeable gaps.

Of course, men are great for closing gaps. We don't like gaps. Gaps are bad. So, I made the decision to buy my wife some shrubbery for her birthday, and thus I stood in the middle of this garden store with nary a clue as to what I needed.

Fortunately, Brad soon appeared to assist me. Brad was a handsome, strapping young lad, and I'm sure the local women enjoyed having Brad tend to their bush and shrub needs. But Brad was not just "beefcake," he was very knowledgeable about his products. Of course, my questions were limited to, "How big does that one get?" I selected a holly-type bush, and Brad suggested I get a male and a female. Apparently, these plants engage in some type of procreating activity. Who knew? I must have missed that lesson in biology class. I had no idea how they accomplished this, but they must do it after dark because I have never, ever, witnessed this hot action and am sure I would remember if I had.

So, I got the two holly "love" shrubs and bought a Korean type plant just in case my wife did not like the other selections. You might say I bought the third plant literally "to hedge my bet." Har, har, double har!

When my wife saw the bushes, she was not pleased. We have our own domains in this marriage, and by my purchase, I had crossed into my wife's landscaping territory. I knew that was a risk but thought that I had the benefit that it was a birthday gift going for me. I was wrong.

She looked scornfully at the holly plants and said I wasted my money because she could easily transplant some from her mother's yard. I'm thinking, "If this was so easy to do, why wasn't it done at any time in the last two years?" Of course, I don't say this out loud because you don't stay married for 30 plus years by actually saying every thought that comes to mind. Do you?

I had prepared for this outcome however. I had told Brad that my wife might not like my choices, and he assured me the shrubs could be returned if not damaged. So, I calmly presented the receipt to my wife and encouraged her to take them back and get what she wanted.

Secretly, I hoped that she would keep them. I had made the trip to the nursery, and I had actually put some effort into my choices. In addition, for some strange reason I was growing fond (har again!) of the Korean one. Now there would have been a time that I might not have wanted my wife to interact with that plant-stud Brad, but it wasn't an issue now.

I believe after the shock wore off, my wife realized that I had tried to do a good thing, and she decided to plant the bushes. She ignored my advice not to plant the Korean one on the north side of the property. My concern was that a North

Korean plot would turn into a communist plant, and I knew from old movies how damaging a communist plant could be to your operation.

So my wife is happy. I am happy. And the bushes appear to be enjoying their new home. I don't know if the male and female have engaged in, well, nature type activity yet, but I'm sure they will when they get to know each other better and the time is right.

Dylan Callens

Dylan Callens began writing for the Laurentian University newspaper, *Lambda*, as a humor columnist, then as the news editor. During that time, he produced his first novel, which, upon completion, promptly found its way to the garbage container. He would have used a recycling bin, except those weren't around at the time. Dylan took a break from writing after university but blasted onto the indie scene with his first novel, *Operation Cosmic Teapot*, a humorous and satirical look at humanism. His second, soon to be released novel, *Interpretation*, promises not to be nearly as humorous.

For updates, check out his website: http://www.cosmicteapot.net *Operation Cosmic Teapot* is available on Amazon: https://www.amazon.com/dp/B018YXFOUK

The Splooge Jar

"You remember Jimmy Biggs, right," Tommy asked, sucking back yet another beer, their table already littered with empties.

George looked up to the ceiling, trying to work out the answer, his head swimming with alcohol, "You mean that nerdy kid from high school?"

"That's the one, only he weren't so nerdy. I mean he was, he was good with computers and all that, but he weren't no real nerd," Tommy waved at the waitress with two fingers. She politely nodded and headed back to the bar.

"Yeah, I remember him. Why?"

"You know, I forgot all about Jimmy but I ran into him the other day. Did you ever hear those stories about him when we were in high school?"

"What stories, you mean?"

"For starters, his last name ain't Biggs. That's a nickname on account he's so big, you know, his cock. Did you know that?"

"No, I never knew that."

"Lotsa hung guys out there, so that ain't the weird part, though. Did you know that he masturbated a lot? I'm talking he's the genuine spunk monkey," Tommy slid a ten dollar bill across the table for the waitress who glared at him when she heard the words *spunk monkey*. Tommy gave her a wink which was returned with a hollow grunt.

"No, I didn't. But that's not so weird. Everyone masturbates a lot in high school. It's part of the process."

"It was more than a process for Jimmy, though. As a teen he was arguing with Henry Longfellow on an hourly, let me tell you. He'd spank it everywhere and anywhere. He couldn't help himself. Whenever he had a moment alone, they say he'd whip it out. But that still ain't the weird part. Did you ever hear that he kept all of his splooge in a jar?"

"What," George looked up from his beer, "There's no way."

"I never believed it either. I heard the story back in the day, but I slushed it off as some schoolyard bullshit. But, apparently he found one of those giant pickle jars laying around in his basement. You know, the kind with the pickled eggs at the end of a low-life bar? Well, he finds this jar and starts thinkin' to himself, 'I gotta do something with it.' So he's in the basement staring at the thing and the urge, you know, comes over him. So he starts crankin' one out. Well, the story is that he came all over the jar and that was his inspiration."

"Let me get this right. Jimmy saved all of his sperm in this jar?"

"After that moment, he did. And with how much he masturbated, he filled it up pretty quick, apparently."

"That's impossible. Those jars hold a gallon."

"They sure do. Now I've done the math on this and let me tell you, it's quite the feat. Try to follow me here, the science is done in that damn metric bullshit. The average amount of goo that a guy shoots out in a standard load is around three milliliters, give or take. Those jars add up to about four thousand milliliters. That means that he masturbated at least one thousand three hundred thirty-three times to fill up the jar."

"That's messed up. It makes me want to vomit a little."

"Oh, it gets worse, let me tell you."

"How can it possibly get worse?"

"He apparently filled that thing up to the brim in under a year. Now he loved that jar so much, he stuck a label on the thing and called it #1," Tommy took a swig, "Then, he goes and finds another. It became an obsession for him to fill up these things."

"How many did he fill up?"

"I'll get to that in a second. Anyway, when Jimmy got outta high school, he ran into some bad luck. He didn't want to go to college and he couldn't find a job. So, he tried going to a sperm bank. He brought two of those jars with him, one in each hand, carrying them down the road like they was cartons of milk or something. Jimmy gets to the sperm bank and sets his jars down on the counter and proudly says to the receptionist, 'I've collected over twenty-four hundred samples for you,' with that big grin that he has. He figures he's in for a huge pay day, thinking that there's at least eighty-four thousand dollars-worth of baby batter there."

"No way. That can't be true."

"That's what he told me when I saw him. Swear to Christ almighty."

George shook his head, laughing, "So, what happened?"

"What the hell do you think happened? The receptionist was horrified. There are two giant jars of splooge that's been stewing for who knows how many years right in front of her. She pushed her chair back a bit so that she weren't so close. Jimmy proudly told her, 'There's more where that came from,' and gives her a wink. Well, the receptionist tries to keep her calm and tells him that they only take fresh samples. You have to be in the sperm bank to provide it. Then she kindly tells Jimmy to take those jars the hell outta there."

"That is pretty gross, you have to admit."

"Oh, I'll admit that, for sure. But what got me was that he said, 'There's more where that came from.' I mean, I started to wonder, just how many jars does this guy have?"

"Did you ask him," asked George corralling all the empties to one side.

"Of course I did. I asked him right after he told me that. And he says that at that point he had four. I said holy shit, that's a lot of twinkie filling. I looked it up, in each milliliter there are one hundred million sperm. That means, on average there are three hundred million. In a jar, that makes over six hundred billion. That's more hamburger's than McDick's has ever served up. And he had four jars like that!"

"What happened after that?"

"He said that he spiraled into depression. He had some shitty jobs working in fast food and crap like that but he'd keep getting fired because he couldn't keep it in his pants all the time. So they'd catch him basting the ham, so to speak. I guess he'd had enough of it and tried to claim disability."

"Disability for what?"

95

"He said that he got a doctor's note that he was addicted to pulling the taffy and couldn't perform normally in society. I don't know what kind of quack would write that up but he did. Well, Jimmy went to the disability office and submitted his note and they laughed him out of there, as you can imagine. But Jimmy really did have a problem."

"He can't get a job and he can't get disability. Sounds like he's going to be homeless."

"You would think so, wouldn't you? But when I saw him, he was getting into a goddamn Porsche."

"He's lifting cars?"

"Not at all. You haven't let me finish. Jimmy found out how to turn this problem of his into gold."

"How did he do that?"

"Well, you remember he was good with computers, right?"

"Yeah. He was kinda nerdy."

"Kinda. But not really. Anyway, one day Jimmy's on his computer. God only knows what he's looking at but the mood strikes him, as it always did, and he starts rubbing himself. So he's going for it, you know. He's looking up at his computer screen and screams Eureka, just as he's coming. A real friggin Archimedes moment if I ever heard one."

"Archimedes?"

"Don't you ever read? Anyway, yeah, he gets this idea that he should set up his own webcam site and Shemp the hog for people. Show everyone his talent and his jars, you know."

"He made his own porn site?"

"Not porn, exactly. Well, yes porn. But all he does is masturbate, collect his sample, and show off his jars. People subscribe to this shit, he says."

"No way. You're telling me that people pay to see him whack off?"

"Apparently they do. He says that he has something like ten thousand subscribers and each of them pay five dollars a month to tune in whenever they feel like it and watch him shake his sausage. Then, like I said, they watch him collect his protein shake. He adds it to his collection of jars, which he says is now a total of ten."

"That's disgusting! Some of that has to be over six years old."

"At least. But I think it sends a good message."

"What message is that? Get rich quick by masturbating?"

"What? No George, of course not. Were you even listening? The message is, do what you love. Always do what you love."

"Sure, Tommy. When I figure out how to get rich by drinking beer, I'll let you know."

Shoshanah Lee Marohn

Shoshanah Lee Marohn is an artist and writer. She lives on a small farm in rural Wisconsin with several goofy looking sheep.

Check out her blog at: http://dommn2703.blogspot.com
See her books at Amazon:
http://tinyurl.com/theArtisticShepherdess

Piano Camp

I can't remember the name of the university where I got my teaching degree. The college has changed its name twice since I went there. I think they wanted to change the name to make the university sound like a place where smart people went, but the actual result is that people like me can't remember where they went to college.

In the summer of 1999, I went to my nameless university's financial aide office to set things up for summer school, and found that I was one credit short of getting a five thousand dollar Pell Grant for the summer.

"You mean I don't get my grant unless I take another summer school credit?"

"Yes," said the kind young man behind the desk. (Everyone was pretty nice there.)

"So if I take one credit, you'll give me five thousand dollars?"

"Yes," he repeated, pulling a summer school course list out of his drawer. "If I were you, I would just sign up for a credit, any credit at all."

A perusal through the course listings showed that there weren't all that many one credit courses. I could take more than one credit, but unnecessary work was not on my summer itinerary. I started looking through the art classes for something easy. No luck. Then the music classes- I had always felt myself to be musical, although I'd never mastered any particular instrument. "Piano Camp" was listed, one credit, and it only lasted a week. I had a little electronic keyboard at home and I had been working my way through *The Complete Piano Player* for the last year or so. Beautiful! Perfect! I would learn to play piano better, and also get my grant in the least painful way possible. The summer was looking good.

Two months later, the first day of piano camp dawned, and the weather was as sunny and bright as my disposition. Since I'd never been to the music building before, I went early to find my classroom. Along the way, I became caught up in a crowd of children with their parents. Huh. Wonder what they were all doing? Field trip? Church group?

All of the children seemed to be headed towards the general direction of my classroom. Why do they always schedule people so close together? I wondered. Here we had a whole empty campus, and they had to schedule some sort of children's program right in the same building as my piano class.

I went to the correct room number and found oodles of people, most of them children, standing in various lines. Not knowing what else to do, I stood in one of the lines, planning on asking the person at the front where my piano class was and why it was listed as this room number? But, as I drew nearer to the front of my queue, the horrible truth became apparent. Little people were leaving the front of the line with tee shirts that said, "Piano Camp, 1999" on them. When I finally got to the front of the line, I was speechless. I was greeted by a smiling man with a very bible-school-youth-group-leader air about him.

"Piano or violin?" he asked me with an uninterrupted grin.

"Um- piano."

"Rooming here or off-campus?"

"Sorry?"

"Are you staying in the dorms?"

"No, no- I-" I owned a house with my husband on the West Side.

"Good. Name?"

"Listen, I thought this was a college class. It's in the summer school course listing."

"Oh, so you're one of our music majors?"

"No, no. I just wanted to learn the piano better." I felt like this was a really lame excuse for being there- oddly, because it was the purpose, wasn't it?

"Oh, you can do that."

"Well, what do the music majors do here? They're learning, right?"

"No, actually, they help our teachers." Help? Help!

"Am I the only adult student, then?"

"Oh, no," he was still smiling. "I'm sure there is someone else. Tee shirt size?"

After having been given my tee shirt, I was then herded into an audition waiting room. Apparently, we were all to be put into different groups according to our ability levels. Looking and the six- and eight-year-olds around me, clutching piano music books, I had a sudden urge to run. But it was five thousand dollars. And I had to take a credit to get my money. Piano camp, as it turned out, started towards the end of the summer and therefore it was too late to begin something easier on the ego, like, say, a four credit Calculus class, or Botany for Physicists. Those classes were probably all full of six-year-olds already, anyway.

It was a brief wait until I was sent into a small room with a grand piano and three skinny, intimidating professors dressed in black. I took a seat at the piano bench. I gave them my name, and they scribbled on clipboards. How was it that you had to audition for a children's piano camp? Every moment, my day was becoming more and more surreal.

"I'm going to sing some notes," said the only woman, "and I would like you to play them, exactly as I sing them, on the piano." It seemed easy enough.

"Okay."

She hummed a little melody. I played it as best as I could, starting on a high G note. The piano didn't play like my electronic keyboard at home; my notes came out all funny, one note strong, one weak, and I realized that my keyboard at home was not touch-sensitive. I had never played a real piano before, and it was obvious to my judges.

The lady who had hummed the melody looked at me disapprovingly, and I assumed it was the uneven volume of my notes. But, no, I was actually inadequate in several areas.

"The melodies all begin on Middle C," she told me, as though I should have known.

"Oh, okay," said I, and I played her little melody again, this time starting on C. The woman stood up and walked over to me.

"*This* is Middle C," she said, and played a C note two octaves down from where I had started. That was a real confidence builder for me. When the audition was over, I was assigned to a group of players "like me."

Every day of piano camp was the same. Piano camp turned out to consist of a week full of mornings in music theory classes, with afternoons full of small group or private lessons, followed by practice with your group for the final performance Friday night.

So there would be a recital. I decided immediately not to reveal the time and place of the recital to anyone I knew, not even to my husband.

I was assigned to be in the same group as four adolescent boys, ranging in age from twelve to fifteen. And there was me, a twenty-seven-year-old woman who worked as a school bus driver during the school year and was studying to be an English teacher.

Most of the boys were at about my same playing level, but there was one, the fifteen-year-old, who was much better than all of us. Why he was in our group was a mystery to me at first, until I figured out that he didn't play classical music. He played rock. He could sing well, too. He's probably playing an Elton John tune in an off-the-strip bar in Las Vegas right now. He was an excellent sight reader, and the choice to not play classical was clearly a choice, and not a matter of inability to do so. Also, this kid carried around a harmonica. He was playing with fire.

For much of piano camp, the fact that there was any other music besides classical music was completely ignored. Interestingly, though, for two afternoons out of five, there was a jazz pianist who was available to give lessons, a man with two Emmys under his belt. My group, led by myself and harmonica boy, were the only ones who took advantage of his lessons. The Great Jazz Pianist Guy wrote out chord progressions instead of notes; clearly he was in league with the devil. Learning licks from him, I could feel my brain growing. With the other teachers, my hands would progressively shake more and more until I wanted to die. With The Great Jazz Pianist Guy, I wanted to sing. Unfortunately, it was only a few hours, but I definitely learned a lot, particularly about the importance of a strong left hand.

Another thing mostly ignored at piano camp was the fact that it is possible to teach one's self music. I guess it's that self-preservation thing. If piano teachers taught you that you could teach yourself to play the piano, they would be putting themselves out of business.

I think harmonica guy and I were the only ones there who didn't have private lessons. The students all played for each other a lot, and time and time again, you could ask someone there why he or she had learned a particular piece of music and the kid would say, "My teacher made me learn it." I couldn't wrap my head around that for anything. For me, music had always been about fun- sometimes even about excessive drinking. Here, it was reduced to drills, simply following notes on a page correctly. Correctly? But what about improvisation?

The second most embarrassing moment of the week (the first would be during the concert, of course) was when the site-reading teacher complimented me. When I was called upon to play, I played a song on the piano for the class, decently, and I was relieved when it was over. But it wasn't over. Lots of questions came from my young classmates. They were curious about my presence. How long had I been playing? Who had taught me? Why did I suck so badly? Stupidly, I answered all of their questions honestly, and it came out that I had no teacher, that I had just been working out of this book for a year, and that I had no real piano. And, obviously, I was an adult.

That did it. According to the woman teaching the class, (the same one who taught me where Middle C was located,) I was a Hero. She stood behind me and gave a speech,

"I find this so inspiring. Let Shoshanah be an example to us all. She has no teacher, she's well beyond the age when we usually start playing an instrument, and she doesn't even have a piano- not even a piano! and yet she's still here, today, learning how to play."

Well... sort of. I blushed. I fumed. I cringed. How could I tell them that I just wanted my Pell Grant? That all of this had been a horrible mistake? That playing the piano was sort of like knitting or making homemade ice cream to me? A hobby. A pastime. But clearly, music meant a whole lot more, although I wasn't ready to admit it right then. I would never be so embarrassed over making a batch of ice cream or knitting a scarf. The lady made me feel like a freak for even considering teaching myself anything. Was I really such an anomaly?

The afternoons of practice were trying for anyone over fifteen and female. The boys and I would be sent off to a practice room with some music which we were expected to practice. The boys would inevitably find some kind of trouble to get into instead of practicing. Part of their horsing around included just playing whatever they wanted, which, I have to admit, was fun. Music is a great equalizer. When we were actually playing music together, it didn't matter who we all were, individually. We were just musicians.

We found out that we liked jamming together. We were each good at a certain part (I played the bass line). The Great Jazz Pianist Guy we had seen for a few hours had given us some good tips. Now that we knew each other, we didn't want to play a classical piece for the concert. We wanted to jam together on stage and play a twelve bar blues. Our best pianist, the fifteen-year-old, didn't even want to play the piano for the recital. He wanted to play his harmonica instead.

By Thursday afternoon, it was apparent that we probably would not be able to play anything but the blues. We hadn't practiced anything that was formally written down. We were just screwing around and having fun. I, in my age and wisdom, had done nothing to encourage the boys to practice classical piano. I convinced them, in fact, that if we played the blues well enough, the powers that be would allow us to play the blues for the concert. So on Thursday, we wrote an arrangement, ran through it a few times, and then two of the boys went to get the head Maestro so we could play it for him.

Ten minutes later, the six of us (the four boys, the Maestro, and I) were stuffed into a tiny room with two grand pianos, and with a, "One two three four!" we played our hearts out for the Maestro. We were on fire. We were bumping into each other, playing over each other's hands, having a good old time. We were exuberant at the end. Sweating. Smiling. We'd done good.

"Well, what do you think? Can we play it for the concert?"

The Maestro (we really had to call him, "Maestro") wore all black and held a white handkerchief in front of his mouth, like a barrier to keep himself separate from the our music. He was not smiling. He hesitated to answer.

"Surely you're not going to count out loud like that during the concert?"

None of us was really used to playing with other people, and in order to stay together, we had been sometimes shouting out, "One two three four one two three four!" to stay together. This had been a suggestion of The Great Jazz Pianist Guy's. But The Great Jazz Pianist Guy was now gone, on to LA for a recording.

"Well, yeah. We were going to count out loud."

"No, no. The audience will hear you! You can't count out loud."

So, we were cleared to play the blues, as long as we did not count out loud.

I was quite happy. I was ready to go home for the day but the boys had other plans.

"Hey, we gotta do this right! We should have costumes!" Oh, no. No. No no no no no no no no.

"No, guys, we don't need costumes," I said. But everyone else was in agreement.

"Yeah, yeah! We should wear all black! We'll be like the Blues Brothers!"

"And sunglasses! Black sunglasses!"

"No, no, boys, I don't think we need sunglasses. That's okay."

"I know I know I know I know I know! We'll have the sunglasses in our hands, and then we'll like line up on the front of the stage, and then right before we play, like, we'll all put on our sunglasses together, like all at the same time!"

"No, really, boys, that's okay. Let's just wear black."

"Oh, that is so awesome! We have to do that!"

"That's bad!" (Bad meant good in the teenaged vernacular.) "Everyone, let's bring our sunglasses tomorrow so we can practice!"

I was now definitely, definitively, indubitably not telling anyone about this performance on Friday.

Friday evening arrived on schedule, in spite of me.

It just so happened that piano camp coincided with a time period when I was briefly addicted to buying completely inappropriate clothing on eBay. Therefore, I had a dress which would, under the normal circumstances of my life, have been inappropriate for anything which I might normally do. Of course, performing a blues number with four teenaged boys was not in my normal realm of activity, and the dress, unlike most of its closet mates, might actually be worn.

This was no ordinary dress. It was black, clingy, and low cut, but that wasn't all this dress was about. The fabric actually sparkled. It had some sort of willowy starlight woven into it. I was 150 pounds and wished I was 130, but the dress would have none of this. The dress said these curves were on purpose, these curves were there for a reason, and the dress knew exactly what these curves were there for, even if I didn't. It was impossible to walk in this dress without a slight seductive sway of the hips. The dress was a performer, and the dress could only be worn for a performance, and the dress insisted on being worn. Who was I to argue?

I met some of the boys' parents in the auditorium that night. They clearly had no idea what to make of me. Child molester in a shimmering black dress? What?

The program had cryptically labeled our act, "Dueling Pianos."

I sat with my band. "Do you have your sunglasses?" They kept asking me.

"Well, yeah, but you know, we don't have to do the sunglasses routine..."

"Yeah, we do."

Sweet Jesus.

We sat in the audience for most of the show. Some of the acts were amazingly bad. Of course, the players were six-year-olds.

By the time our act was up, my palms were sweating. We walked up the stairs to the stage. (I heard a lady say, "nice dress.") We stood in a line facing the audience, the boys all in black and me conspicuously grown up and in an evening gown. Then, on cue, we all put on black sunglasses at exactly the same time. There were chuckles in the audience. We gave each other a quick and serious nod (I have no idea where that came from) and took our places in front of the grand pianos.

We started playing out of time with one another. We had never played together without counting out loud. Screw the Maestro! As the bass line, it was my duty to keep us all together. I started yelling, "One two three four one to three!" and the boys started counting with me, one by one. And then we were together, just like that. A miracle. We were good. Playing over each other's hands and sweating and smiling and having a good old time. And our best pianist stopped playing, stood up, grabbed a mike, and pulled out his trusty harmonica and started tearing it up. And for a few minutes there, to be completely honest, I was having a good time.

The piano camp recital was reviewed on the last page of the newspaper the next day. Of all of the performers, we were the only ones mentioned by name. We had made an impression. I don't remember the specifics, now, except for one detail: they spelled my name so horribly wrong that no one could ever possibly know I was there. Complete anonymity! I hadn't even told any friends about it. It was my secret week of piano camp. Until now.

Meaghan Curley

Utica, NY writer, Meaghan Curley is a member of the Utica Writers Society and the Humor Writers of America. She once won a poetry contest with a poem about how much she hates poems.

Follow Meaghan on Twitter – https://twitter.com/CRAYOLATIMEMEAG
Follow Meaghan on Facebook – https://www.facebook.com/meaghan.curley

The CARF Crisis

Who would have guessed? With all the thousands upon thousands of Apocalypse theories circulating (zombies, hydrogen bombs, nuclear annihilation, North Korea, Donald Trump) that it would end like this—Death by Fangirls?

It happened early, like 9/11. But the damage and depravity that lasted long afterwards was reminiscent of the sacking of Rome. Only with way more Goths.

On the day, AR-Day, adults all over the city trying to leave for work were shocked to find scores upon scores of teens, young adults and 25-plusers languishing in the streets. Sobbing in each other's arms like inconsolable debris, people at first assumed this was another anti-war-student-protest ("Get back to your bong, hippies!" 30-year-old-plusers would cry, angry that they weren't allowed to just drive over these irritable speed bumps and were forced to walk to work and be reminded about how out-of-shape they were).

They checked the news though. There weren't any congressional proposals for war. No State of the Unions, no big addresses from Obama (just silly pictures of him trying to learn how to use Snapchat for the first time. Lol #geezerprez). A couple mentions of ISIS but college students hated them too, so what's the problem?

Nobody knew and not due to lack of effort. Neighbors, parents, psychologists, even firefighters tried talking to the legions of lachrymose ladies (and Steve) to delineate the cause of their strife. It was impossible to understand them though with their open-mouthed weeping, their extended throat guttural noises, and their shrill cries of pain.

Eventually, the older-adults were tempered by impatience and they were sick of using personal days because it would be 'illegal' to drive over, what they considered to be, overly dramatic 'children'.

So, they called the cops and, like every other time the police were involved as of recent, it went from sugar to shit. Quick.

Four days later 85% of Utica, New York looked like the beleaguered ruins of Alexander's Library (in the CARFs defense though, 40% of Utica was already abandoned and half-dilapidated thanks to hard-pressed economies so most of what they vandalized and set on fire were merely corner stores and foreclosed homes).

When the mayor said 'fuck this' and abandoned office, many people followed. Those who could, went to New Hartford. Those who didn't want to pay New Hartford taxes, chose Whitesboro. Those who weren't racist but were still too poor for New Hartford, went to Rome. A couple of groups said 'fuck this altogether' and disbanded for Canada.

The rest stayed. Too poor to move, too American to be Canadian, and too loyal to watch Utica be ransacked by CARFs, a secret forces was born out of this crisis. The anti-CARFs prerogative was obvious, but nonetheless reckless: stop the spread of the CARF. Just like 'Nam. Only instead of General Westmoreland, they had a black haired blue-dreaded female named Ann.

And instead of fighting communism, they were fighting a much more dangerous enemy; they were fighting Crazy Alan Rickman Fans, four days after the news unfurled the truth that would damage them all to the very core—their God is dead.

On the fifth day, in an abandoned heroin den just across the street from the County Office Building, one of the Anti-CARFs was positioned in wait. With death-like stillness, one ear against the door and one eye squinting tirelessly into the peephole, she held guard.

By mid-day, the sound of scuffling inside tin jolted the rigid person alive. In an instant, she pried the door open, leaning half her body out the door, before immediately receding inside. This time holding a package. The people who were dispended in abject silent almost rejoiced with religious zeal at the sight of the orange mailer. No one went to snatch the package from the retriever. Instead, they all waited with bated breath as she handed it over to their leader with blue dreads.

She practically ripped it entirely to shreds before revealing what they had hoped to come: a black, hooded sweatshirt, customized and ordered online. The female named Ann held the hooded sweatshirt up, exalted, showing it to her colleagues.

"I can't believe it came!" One of the anti-CARFs exhaled joyously.

"I told you!" Ann replied with a chained-link fence smile. "Neither snow nor rain nor heat nor End of the World keeps those mailman from delivering their mail!"

But the smiles wouldn't last. Action had to be taken.

Gathered around her like occult followers, their faces bent and eerie blue from the glow of their smartphones, members of the anti-CARFs sped through their questions one last time:

"When...was he born?"

"February 21st, 1946."

"What…is his full name?"

"Alan Sidney Patrick Rickman."

"Name five movies he was in."

Ann opened a heavily pierced mouth to answer when another person challenged, "Besides *Harry Potter* and *Die Hard*."

A couple people in the room made audible gasps ("Alan Rickman was in other shit?!"). Ann teethed one of her lip rings as she thought. Everyone went dead quiet as she separated her perforated lips and answered with confidence,

"*Dogma, the Song of Lunch, Rasputin: the Dark Servant of Destiny, Love Actually* and *Perfume: the Story of a Murderer.*"

"Ooh! You referenced an *HBO* special AND a *PBS* special! Nice!" Congratulated her interrogator, giving Ann a deserved high-five.

A couple of the Anti-CARFs cheered but not Brandon, the man who made the last question so difficult. Waiting in the corner of the room like a cockroach hiding until the lights went off, a middle-aged man stood with folded arms pressed against himself. Long sleeves concealed the track marks that would have revealed that even before the CARF Crisis began he had spent many days in this very room, deprived of sunlight or food.

Hedonistic, hazel eyes sent hot piercing looks into the back of Ann's wild hairstyle as he spoke above the cheers:

"But is it enough to trick those fangirls?"

119

"And Steve." Added one of the other men.

Brandon rolled his eyes but relenting added, "And that one weird fanboy." Stepping from the corner he walked over towards Ann and from his first step over, Ann glared at him with her heavy eyelinered eyes. Her lips squeezed together so close that all four of her rings clanked together, making a small clink of disdain before Brandon added, "How do we know they won't see through your bullshit?"

"Because we understand what's fueling their pain now." Ann remarked, her clenched fists tugging against her black, ripped sleeves.

"So we're just supposed to *hope* that they *think* you sympathize with them?" Brandon retorted, cruelty in his voice crystalized by rancor and his own indulgent pain.

"I *do* sympathize." Ann implored, her voice hard.

"It doesn't matter." A window guard nicknamed Grub replied, peering anxiously through the peepholes of a barracked window. "They'll be coming soon. This is our last shot."

The group members moved into position. They started preparing their weapons, gathering the clothes they would need, began filtering water from the orange-toilet bowl in hopes it would be drinkable once war comes.

As Ann threw on the hooded sweatshirt, one of the supporters held out a bag of chips for her to take. It was the last of what they had. Another reason this wasn't optional anymore, it was detrimental.

"Wait twenty minutes, then try finding me. I'll try to keep them downtown."

"How will we know if you're in?" He asked.

"They have guns. You'll hear if I don't."

A young woman, no older than 30, said that. Not because she was reckless or thought herself invincible but because it's easy to overcome the fear of Death when you and your friends are starving.

Saying her 'goodbyes' (and a silent 'fuck you' to Brandon), Ann zipped up her winter coat, threw on a hat, ran through the back, passing by an overturned oven and stomping down the floors that held layers upon layers of grime, graffiti and broken needles and travelled out through the basement cellar.

Even in low-January sun, the light burned her raccoon eyes and she hissed at it like a Goth-kid stereotype as she stumbled back into the Utica streets.

She looked around but saw only barrenness. The cold streets were bleached from snow and ice. She was pleased to see that someone in the city was respectful enough to pick up all the corpses of those who decided to go out like Hans Gruber and fling themselves from the tallest building they could find (in their case, the Utica State Office Building which possessed only seventeen stories instead of their preferred 35 stories but none the less it got the job done).

Ann continued upward from downtown. She tightened her legs, feeling as if her solitary footfalls beat against the ground like conspicuous bleeps on radar detectors. She squirmed in her coat, chewing on her metal rings.

Where were they? Tracking had given them the impression that they congregated in front of the Court Houses around high noon. Minutes edged by, like eons to a volcano, all while asking, where's the boom?

Then, like trash caught in an updraft, they came with the wind. Ann had stopped walking long enough to readjust her sleeves to protect her frozen hands when she could heard the charming sounds of a handgun switching its safety off.

Ann picked up her head to see a staggering amount of weapons being pointed at herself: hardly any guns; mostly kitchen knives, or tools, she noticed a ton of crowbars and hammers, even some women brandishing upside-down brooms where the handle had been improvised as a spear.

Without a second thought, she rose her arms high and wide above her head, submitted to her knees and screamed, "Don't kill me! Don't kill me!"

They fashioned a circle in the middle of the street but once she surrendered, they tightened themselves despite their numbers. Eighty of them enclosed, barely occupying half of the vacuous street they ruled over.

If Ann took the time, she would have recognized some faces: Some from long-forgotten school days, some from the more recent days frequented in rehab. But she focused on one face. One that stood straight ahead of her, holding the pistol she heard with two hands, wearing a wrinkled, dirtied Hottopic shirt bearing her idol's in his most famous role. *Save me, wizard bro*! She prayed.

"Who are you?" The Head CARF demanded, her voice bouncing off of the hollowed street like a dog's bark.

Ann could feel her conversational powers drying up. How did action heroes do this? She asked herself. How can they be so charming with a gun threatening to blow their fucking face to shreds?

"She's speechless," she heard a voice from behind tell Al.

"You're right. Anybody that's scared of us is clearly not one of us. Kill her." She ordered.

Suddenly she remembered English. "No-no-no! Wait-wait-wait! I am one of you! I am!"

"Bull pizzle!" One of them who was closer to her own age shouted. "She's not a CARF! She's probably a David Bowie Fan!"

"No! No! I can prove it!" She implored. Peach-colored palms were the closest she had to white flags. Al gestured to her phalanx to allow her to (killers and thieves always give the moribund their last chance). The crew let her continue but held onto their weapons harder. Ann fumbled for the coat's zipper and in the most unsteady hand pulled it down. Pushing the garment aside to reveal her chest, she disclosed the hoodie she wore. On it was their God's likeness, looking up, seated at a closed piano that carried books on top, sneering openly at the viewer, bearing teeth in an Ibsen scene.

It was such an obscurity of him that none of them spoke right away so Ann chanced: "I've been in mourning for the last couple of days. I came out today because I heard there were others who understood my pain. I want to join you."

It wasn't the craftiest lie but it was plausible. A few of the CARFs eyes rounded with softness but looked to their leader to gage how they should feel. Red eyes showed she was not assuaged.

"*She's lying.*"

The blood in her face coagulated.

"You do not know our pain!" She bellowed, her voice loud enough to be carried straight to the Heavens, telling their God his disciples would not be tricked. "I know who you are! You are the ones who stayed! Who stayed so they could try and destroy us! But we're not falling for your bullshit tricks!"

124

Ann opened her mouth to try and change her mind but Al charged after her, propelling her gun closer and closer to her face until her bottom lips rings almost tapped the metal end of her barrel.

"Don't. Lie. To. Me."

Fuck, she thought panicking, *they're using direct quotes now! Abort! Abort!*

"*Who—are—you*?" Al barked, her voice heated but slow like lava trailing down the north face of a volcano.

Ann could see her own eyes in the barrel. Makeup still perfect but tears on edge ready to make the corpse she'd leave behind ugly.

"My name is Ann." She confessed at last. "And I am *not* a CARF."

Al's back straightened, casting down at her looks of foulest loathing, unintentionally reminiscent of his idol's more iconic role in that moment. She turned around and was a second away from signaling to her troops to kill when Ann spoke up again,

"But I *do* feel for you guys."

The allegation was so powerful it made Al stop abruptly mid-step. She turned to Ann and saw that she was openly weeping.

"You guys—you guys think that no one gets what you guys are going through. Y-you guys think that this grief you feel, this unrelenting hurt that all of you think is never going to end, is yours and yours alone. But it's not." Sobbed Ann, first to Al and then to the rest. "You guys grew up with this guy. H-he's been a part of your lives longer than most of your family members. And—and I get it. I get it." (Bending her head down, looking into her hands, seeing a part of his sneering face in the corner of her eye she continued) "I bet a lot of you figured him to be...one of the only men in your lives that never hurt you."

With the exception of Al, many of the CARFs arms wavered at her conjecture. Their faces cracking with feelings of grief anew. Ann wasn't bullshitting early. She understood how absorbing bereavement is.

"And—and I get that." Ann went on, her own voice cracking under the weight of strong emotion. "Don't think that the world doesn't get that. But this isn't the way to honor him."

A violent virus shook Al to the bones at hearing this that she bulleted at Ann and pistol-whipped the female until she collapsed underneath herself, bleeding and crying harder.

"YOU—DON'T—TELL—US—HOW—TO—HONOR— HIM!" Al screeched with divine like wrath into Ann's ears. "YOU DIDN'T LOSE SOMEONE HERE, YOU LYING TWAT NUGGET! WE DID!

"Many people have lost!" Ann fired back, unable to move yet unable to be silenced. She could barely yank her chin down, to get a better look at this CARF but managed and said,

"You are not the only one who lost someone you'd never met, Al!"

Al froze at the sound of her own name. Looking down into Ann's face, she was steeled to see unyielding truth behind those raccoon eyes.

"How do you know my name?"

Ann glared at her now. Even though she lied, bloodied and smeared with dirt, her blue dreads spread around her like reverence. With her black arms draped against a bleached white street and her matching clothes flattened as if on purpose, she looked like the martyr of a tenebristic image held in the hearts of only Catholicism's most Hell-obsessed minds. Except for on this holy demon, her chest bore not blood or flame but the almighty gaze of Alan fucking Rickman.

"I know all about you Al. I know you have a shitty drug-addict dad that left when you were baby and died three years ago. I know many of you have your share of daddy issues. And I know you all secretly wanted nothing more than for that man to come to this sordid, sorry excuse for a city and either adopt, fuck or just plain rescue you." (On her right, Steve broke down into big fat baby tears.)

"It's been hard." Ann continued. "On everyone. But you can't let your grief destroy others."

"Why shouldn't we?" Snapped Al, shamelessly crying at this point. Many of them were crying, but unlike them, whose

127

voices cracked and dissolved from ennui, her voice was like a rag soaked in gasoline. "Why? Why shouldn't others feel what we feel?"

Ann was able to prop herself onto her elbows and in the process her black sleeves were scrunched up exposing her forearms. On the skin, trails of the ugliest looking ant mounds scatters across bruised, but healing veins. Al flinched seeing them, not because they were grotesque but because they instigated flashes. Ann saw that flinch. She wasn't surprised.

Looking her dead in the eye, she answered her question:

 "Because that's not how life works, Al." She paused, scanning down the rest of the CARFs, adding, "And I know he taught you guys better than that."

She pinned them down the legion of ladies (and Steve) with cruel truths, leaving the forgotten, abused products of selfish fathers humbled on that empty Genesee Street that they thought they could own.

Many of them succumbing to their anguish. Dropping their weapons, CARFs began to buckle under the plentitude of their pain. Even Al, who still stood over Ann, crumbled into tears and fell to the ground beside her.

Ann was able to sit up and embraced the young woman, who except her comfort and cried into her dreads.

"It's just not fair!" Al howled. "Fucking he has to die but Michael Gambon gets to walk fucking walk around after fucking up the *Goblet of Fire*!? It's just not fair!"

Ann petted the young woman's head, cooing and validating,

"Yes, it is completely unfair."

Al continued to weep openly in her former foe's arms. Ann was still smoothing out the fly-aways on top of Al's head when her chest expanded and she let out one, loud and clear,

"NOW!"

Before Al could even gasp, she was greeted with the sounds of a dozen safety clips clicking off. She picked up her head from Ann's shoulder to find her and her own army entrapped. Except for instead of a couple guns, some household objects and blunt objects, it was all guns being pointed at them.

In one swift motion, Al went from looking over Ann's shoulder to Ann shouldering her in the face, breaking her nose and sending slobbering Al into the ground, bloodied and crying even harder.

Ann stood over her and decreed, "Alan Rickman? More like Al got dicked, *man*."

Contrary to what everyone told her in the den, Ann thought that quip was genius. Everyone cringed. She didn't care. Turning to a disgruntled Brandon, she ordered, "Take them away boys."

"We can't. We're felons." He replied, rolling his eyes. But he made the call beforehand and within minutes, Genesee Street was alive again as patrol cars, buzzy radios and the loud exalts of a mayor who couldn't believe his city was free once more.

"I can't thank you enough Miss Ann!" the Mayor cried, shaking her arm with such brio she was afraid one of her scabs would tear open anew. "Your bravery and your quick-wit will not go unnoticed, Miss Ann!"

In a moment of uncommon happiness she unleashed a smile that radiated beneath her metallic mods. "Thank you, sir."

The mayor let go of her arm long enough for her to roll back down her sleeve. The pair watched as dozens of women (and one hysterical man) squeeze into the backs of several police cars before the mayor broke their comfortable silence to ask uncomfortable question.

He caught sight of her hoodie, and the dead man's stereotypical sneer made him smile.

He chuckled. "You know I didn't even know who that guy was until all this went down. But I guess this whole crisis proved just how popular his character was."

The warmth in Ann's face disappeared hearing that casual confession. He had no idea how disrespectful that was to her. She looked down at a sleeve that most would see as the hidden shame of a pathetic junkie. But she knew (and maybe

He) that wasn't true. Not anymore. They were the wounded skin cells of old. Skin cells that she promised five days ago would regenerate and heal. Giving her arms a chance to be clean, to be the arms of someone good, someone worthy.

Be the arms of someone that a dead Alan Rickman could be proud to see never filled with needles again.

Hákon Gunnarsson

Hákon Gunnarsson was born in Iceland in 1970. A few years later he learned to read and entered the world of books. His head has been there pretty much since then. He has written fiction, but also about cinema, and literature. As for jobs, he has stacked fish, sliced cheese, re-stacked papers, and watched paint dry, but his dogs will tell you that his main job is to walk them.

Visit his Goodreads Author page – https://www.goodreads.com/author/show/7102471.H_kon_Gunnarsson

The Ballad of the Fire Spewing Dragon

Once upon a time there lived a dragon called Ignitabulum. That in itself isn't remarkable because at that time there were a lot of them in the world. I want to tell you the story of this particular dragon because I knew him. He was magnificent to look at. I'll always remember his bright red body. The scales sparkled as if he had just risen from the depths of a lake, and his four wings were powerful. His eyes were black, and deep like bottomless caves. Because the black claws had red stripes it looked like he had ripped someone apart. And believe me, Ignitabulum knew how to do that, and how to spew fire as well. In fact, he had a degree in both from prominent masters.

You see, for years he roamed from place to place, learning from the best dragons in the field. He first sought out a dragon in Geatland. I don't know his name because Ignitabulum never told me what it was. Anyway, that was his first teacher. The one who taught him how to look over a hoard of treasure. Then a thief stole one of the teacher's cups, and everything kind of went up in flames. Ignitabulum's exact words were: "That blasted king Beowulf, and his sidekick Wiglaf killed him." When the young dragon saw his mentor die, he knew it was time to look for new learning grounds. Dead masters don't teach a lot, except maybe: don't let this happen to you.

The battle frightened Ignitabulum, and he ran off to Iceland, where he found his next master. For some years he was the apprentice of the less well-known Lagarfljot Worm who taught him to hide. If any dragon knew the art of hiding, it was him. He was so good at it that for years and years people debated if he was real or not. It wasn't until years later that Wolf's brother proved Lagarfljot Worm was real by capturing him in a work of art. By then Ignitabulum had long since moved on. In a way he had to. One morning he just couldn't find his master, no matter how hard he searched the place.

Ignitabulum's thirst for knowledge wasn't quenched, so he continued his journey. Next he was Fafnir's apprentice. He worked as well as any industrious student could, and soaked himself in every possible speck of knowledge. But, just before

134

he was ready for his final exam, he lost a master. This time because Sigurd killed Fafnir. Once again, he was without a mentor. After losing three masters, and two of them in such a bloody way the young dragon knew that the job he wanted was dangerous. The world was full of evildoers who wanted nothing more than to kill any innocent, but successful dragon.

Despite the dangerous nature of the job, he was quite sure this was what he wanted to do with his life. The goal was clear. He would at some point lie on a great hoard of treasure, eat tasty virgins for breakfast, fight greedy wandering knights and other thieves. So he continued to acquire knowledge from other famous dragons. Next he went to see... Well, let's not get into all that. You see, they were fifty-nine in all. If I would list all the mentors this young dragon sought out, this story would soon turn into nothing but the who's who of the dragon world.

So let's skip the next few years of his life and go forward to the time when he had enough knowledge to tackle the job. With his latest diploma in hand, he bid the master farewell, and went into the world as a fully qualified dragon. Ignitabulum was going to get a cave full of gold, and defend it with all his might. That was a dream, and he was going to live it, but then he ran into a slight problem. You see, the young dragon was not only among the most industrious student in all things related to being a dragon that had ever roamed the Earth. He was also the tiniest one. In fact, he was so small that he could perhaps cover a single gold ring with his body, but you would have had a hard time finding him on top of a great hoard of treasure.

For some reason, call it congenital optimism, call it madness, call it what you will, but he had never thought about his size. It was only after he started to try to get a footing in his chosen profession that it became a big problem. Ignitabulum did everything by the book. He tried what he could to get a hold of a treasure. Went into battle after battle. Threatened to destroy whole kingdoms. And it got him nothing. The day he hit rock bottom was when he broke into a castle, and at the sight of him the king took out of the fly swatter.

That was it. Ignitabulum fell into the bleakest of depression after the incident. His moral decline soon became visible on the outside. Not without a reason because he stopped cleaning himself, slept in ditches and the once shiny red body, turned grey-pink. He looked terrible, and felt worse. And he just bummed about without any direction, saw darkness, and despair everywhere. All his great knowledge was in vain, just because he wasn't the right size.

The shock had hit him so hard that he'd lost interest in everything, including seeking out new knowledge, or even talking to other dragons. One time he passed the Midgard Serpent, and didn't even greet his famous colleague. What would have been the point? They were not colleagues. He knew that. They wouldn't be colleagues until he had a treasure someone wanted, or someone feared him, or at least knew his name. All these famous dragons had accomplished something, while he had at best escaped a fly swatter. His colleagues were the common houseflies, all of which were anonymous.

One night he was flying somewhere, he didn't know where, and didn't care. By accident, he flew straight into a tree branch, and fell into a beer glass which someone had left outside a tavern. For the first time in his life he got drunk. He would have drowned in the beer if the tavern keeper had not been outside gathering the glasses. The tavern keeper took the glass, saw that something was in it, and fished it out. When he realized what he had in his hands, it sent a cold chill up his spine. Memories of the dragon that had burned down his childhood village came to mind. He almost threw the little thing into the trash, but the dragon was so pathetic that he just couldn't find it in himself to do it.

Instead, he put the dragon down on the rag he had for cleaning the tables. It took some time, but the little dragon came to. He coughed up some sparks, and almost set the rag on fire. The tavern keeper cursed: "Bloody dragons," but managed to prevent the fire from spreading. Then the dragon stood up, and tried to fly away, but the tavern keeper caught him. He took the dragon into the house, stopped at the bar, and looked around scratching his beard. Then he turned and went into the kitchen. After some thought he figured out how to turn the sink into a temporary prison for the dragon. As he walked out of the kitchen, he said to himself: "What the hell am I going to do with a drunken miniature dragon?"

The next morning the dragon woke up with a terrible headache. He rubbed his head with one wing while blinking his eyes, trying to get his world into focus. When he tried to walk his feet didn't like the idea.

"How are you little fellow?" asked the tavern keeper without expecting an answer, but got one just the same.

The voice of the dragon was almost inaudible, but because the place was quiet at this time of the day the tavern keeper heard what he said. "My head hurts. It's splitting. What happened? Am I dying?"

This surprised the tavern keeper, but he didn't allow himself to lose face over it. "You've just got a hangover little one."

The dragon fixed his gaze on the tavern keeper, and asked: "Who are you?"

"I'm the owner of this establishment, Mike Matthews."

All Ignitabulum could say was: "Oh," before he vomited.

Mike waited wide-eyed while Ingitabulum recovered. He had seen plenty of people get sick after using too much of his beer, but never a dragon. After what seemed like a long time Ignitabulum finally stopped vomiting, and sat down. They started to talk and dragon told him about his problems. Then

Mike laughed, and offended Ignitabulum, but apologized so the dragon continued his story. Mike began to understand the problems that the dragon was facing. Because the dragon had fallen into his beer glass, he felt some responsibility for the little one. In fact, this was perhaps the first one that had gotten drunk in the tavern, which Mike had ever felt responsible for, so he said: "Well, little one..."

"My name is Ignitabulum."

"All right then. Ignitabulum it is. Anyway, you can stay here if you want."

"Well, I can't do much else being stuck in this... cage."

"I'll let you out."

And even after Mike let him loose from his prison Ignitabulum stayed. For a while he thought it wasn't so bad to live in a tavern. He flew about, and every day he got something to eat. Okay, there may not have been any virgins in his diet, but at least it was food. The only thing was that when customers arrived, he always stayed out of sight in the kitchen. He and Mike had talked about this, and thought it would be safer. It was difficult to predict the feelings of the guests towards him. After all, he was a dragon who could burn things by breath alone.

Over time he began to look better. The colour turned from the sickly, grey-pink, to the healthy, shiny red. He wasn't a great dragon sitting on a massive hoard of treasure, but at least he had a roof over his head. A home, but not a career. That's was what he had. This sometimes made him feel unsuccessful. His life hadn't turned out the way he had hoped it would. Why had he spent years and years studying for a role he would never play? In short, what kind of life was it for a dragon to stay hiding in a tavern? Always being at the mercy of the tavern owner. It bothered him that he had no role, and less security than he wanted. Sometimes at night he had dreams of frying knights, but he never woke up to that reality.

One morning Mike sat in the kitchen, having just finished eating his porridge, and wanted to smoke. He filled the bowl of his pipe, then put it in his mouth and took a test draw to make sure the airflow was good enough. Then he searched his pockets for matches, and cursed. Before he managed to lay the pipe down on the table, Ignitabulum came flying, and said: "You do not need matches. I can light it for you."

Mike watched the dragon fly, then put the pipe back in his mouth. Ignitabulum landed on the rim of the bowl, and blew a flame that was no larger than the flame of a match into the tobacco. Mike looked at the tobacco, and said: "Ignitabulum, let the fire die out, and then do it again, but this time don't aim at one place. Let the flame go all over the tobacco, you know, in an even motion."

The dragon did that, and soon enough Mike was enjoying his pipe. He scratched his beard, and said: "Well, my little monster, who knew you could actually be useful."

The dragon had got a job at last. He'd became a lighter long before anyone had invented such a device. Every time Mike took his pipe, Ignitabulum was ready, willing, and waiting to light it up for him. This became part of their morning routine. After breakfast the tavern keeper prepared his pipe, stuck it in his mouth, and waited for the dragon to come flying to light it up. Sometimes Ignitabulum even sat on the pipe while Mike smoked.

This went on for some months before the tavern keeper got an idea. Instead of having the dragon hiding in the kitchen all the time, why not use him to advertise the place? So he changed the name of the tavern from The White Horse to The Red Dragon. He paid an artist to paint a new sign with the name of the tavern and an image of the dragon spewing fire. When Mike explained his new business plan to Ignitabulum, the little one wasn't sure if he liked it. But he went along with it because he felt he owed the tavern keeper for taking him in when he had nowhere to go. What the little dragon had to do was to create an atmosphere, and light the pipes of the patrons. The tavern keeper introduced the dragon to the regulars one evening, and got loud responses. Some drew swords, others just got quite verbal:

"Why should we take a chance like that. He could burn the whole village down."

"You should be ashamed of yourself."

"Traitor."

"Calm down. Calm down. Just look at this cute, little, red creature. Do you seriously think he could burn down a house, let alone a village?" answered Mike. "He wouldn't even hurt a fly."

Mike was, and still is, one of my best friends. I frequented his fine establishment at that time on a daily basis. Despite that, I'll just admit that I was not convinced. I did not trust dragons. Period. Ever. As in never. Ever. And I made myself clear on the subject. Quite well I think. But as time passed he started to grow on me, and all of us. Sometimes he would sit with me while I drank and I did not even bother to try to swat him. In the end I grew to like the little creature, and for some reason he warmed to me. So much in fact that he told me his story.

Over time he became a part of our community. For a while it happened now and then that the little fellow startled new guests that had not heard of him. Some drew their swords, others became loud, but everyone got the same answer: "If you don't like my friend, you can find another tavern."

As a commercial decision this was right on the money. The place became famous for the little dragon who helped the guests by lighting their tobacco. The Red Dragon was unique because of him, and tourists started to make detours just to visit him. Ignitabulum was a bit shy of his new-found fame to begin with, but soon he was flying from table to table all night, helping anyone that needed fire. He was even ready to pose for traveling artists that wanted to recreate his image on paper. But he always demanded a fee for posing for drawings.

Several years passed. By then Ignitabulum had a small box on a shelf in which lay the few gold coins he had collected. He often sat there when he was not working as a lighter. At that moment he had, in the literal meaning of the word, found his shelf. Life couldn't be better. The tiny dragon would never be as large as his masters, his fame limited, and his hoard of treasure small, and yet he felt it had turned out better than he'd hoped.

For a while at least. I know now that the warning signs were there. Everything seemed good, peaceful, and perfect. That could never have lasted into a happily ever after bliss. There was always the chance that something was lurking around the corner. And it was. When Ignitabulum was finally happy in his new role as a lighter, the king made a royal proclamation about a smoking ban.

Elaine Fields Smith

Elaine Fields Smith is an author and poet living in Central Texas. An ex-nontattooed biker chick, she now loves to ride around in her convertible on four wheels. Her circle of friends is always a source of great material and her first book, Ridin' Around, is a collection of wild and crazy stories.

See her books on www.blazingstarbooks.com

Six at Six

Little ol' lonesome me stepped into the busy restaurant and asked for a table for six. At six. I was there to meet up with five of my college girlfriends and arrived early to get a table. Trouble was it was only twenty minutes until six. So the hostess must have thought there was plenty of time to get a table ready because she motioned to a bench against the front window and advised me to take a seat. That really didn't make sense as there were at least a dozen empty tables within sight of the presently assigned seating area. This was a maroon, diamond tucked bench stretching ten feet long. Seemed more appropriate for the long wait at a dignified steak and potato place rather than at a trendy Mexican joint. But back to the table situation. I was bettin' the bulk of the wait staff didn't go on duty until six, even on a Friday night. Apparently one isn't allowed to sit at a table if there isn't a wait person available to cater to your needs.

People comin' into the place seemed a bit on the grumpy side with sweat runnin' down their necks after being outside in the heat. Still, it wouldn't kill 'em to smile a little. If not at me, at least at each other. Or maybe it would kill 'em, much like the Mexican food they were about to inhale before going back out in the summer swelter. The thought crossed my mind maybe this wasn't the best place for my group to meet. Should have gone for something cool. But finding a restaurant with tables, ice cream, and, most importantly, margaritas ain't all that easy.

Or, maybe those grumpy folks were just plain ornery. For example: after the woman walked toward the restroom, the hostess showed up to seat the men. One laughed sarcastically and said, "Don't tell her where we are!" Now, that is ornery. I'd kick that son of a gun in his hairy shins which should have been covered up with denim instead of sticking out in front of God and everybody from those wrinkled shorts.

Six more minutes passed toward getting my table for six at six. There I still sat on the diamond tucked bench. Luckily, the air conditioning was set on about fifty-five degrees, but I was gettin' a little thirsty. Maybe, I thought, the night shift will come shuffling in and I can get a glass of water while I wait. But no such luck. No new workers appeared. I considered waltzing over to the bar, and demanding loudly, "Gimme some water, easy on the ice." But that was a laugh because there was no way in heaven and earth I would sashay up to the bar with all those young, beautiful people hanging about with their lemon-raspberry flavored malt beverages.

Then again, what's stopping me? If I did go dive in amongst those youngsters, I would grin and nod as though we knew each other, and they'd think I was some crazy old lady. Though, I am happy to say not much gray shows in my decently brown hair and I have never colored it. In fact, I recently sat in a group of twenty-three high school girlfriends and was pretty sure only myself and one other gal had not resorted to washing away the gray. She had plenty and was proud to have it. As my daddy used to say, I'd rather it turn gray than turn loose.

Regardless, this old age thing is mostly in the mind, partly in the body. I recently read somewhere that the average person considers "old age" to be at least ten years over their current age. I find this to be true. Those twenty-two year old beautiful people probably would think this fifty-nine year old to be elderly. But they'd be dead wrong. Not me. No siree. What they don't know is I drive a fast car, have a motorcycle license, and also own a fine looking convertible. Sure, most of my friends are not only parents, but grandparents, but I skipped that extra contributor that would certainly have forced massive amounts of Loving Care into my hair.

As it got closer to six, the six hadn't shown up yet. Did I worry they wouldn't and I'd still be sittin' by my lonesome self at six-thirty at a table for six-if I ever get one, that is. No, I wasn't concerned. I knew the other five would come and make us six. But as time passed, I thought more seriously about that glass of water. Or just some ice. Just as I rose to take action on that idea, one of my friends entered the restaurant. It struck me funny or ironic that it is the gal who lives the farthest away. I thought, if she wants some water, too, perhaps we can face the beautiful people together over at that bar and say something like, "Bartender," slam our fists down on the polished wood, "I need a drink...of water."

Mehreen Ahmed

Queensland writer, Mehreen Ahmed has been publishing since 1987. Her writing career began with journalism and academic reviews and articles. Her journalistic articles appeared in Sheaf, a campus newspaper for the University of Saskatchewan Canada between 1987-1999. Later on, she published fiction, mostly introspective.

See her work on Amazon -- amazon.com/author/amazon.com.mehreenahmed

Charade

The three friends, Una, Ulle and Ursula had more things in common than the initial 'U,' in their names. In all likelihood, it was believed that while Una was a bit shy, Ulle was not and Ursula, the happy medium, was perfectly poised between the two. Ulle's vivacity sometimes angered Una to the hilt. One day, they went out to have coffee. As they were looking for a place to sit down, Una said haltingly that she wanted to sit at the far end of the room. This enraged Ulle.

"You're really awkward, you know, and why can't we sit in the middle?"

"Because, I'm embarrassed."

"Who do you think, in their right mind, would look at you?"

"Maybe, no-one."

"Still, you're the way you *are*. You will not change."

"I can't change. You should know that by now."

"Now, now let's not waste time arguing over seats," Ursula chimed in. "Why can't we all sit in that corner next to the wall. It would be the best of both worlds?"

They nodded in agreement. Through the crowded restaurant, they walked towards the semi-dark corner. Una sat down with her back towards the people so she didn't have to look at them. And, vice versa, Ulle sat grudgingly opposite her with Ursula in the middle. Once settled in their chairs, they ordered coffee with orange almond, which they all loved so much. Their differences were soon forgotten and they began to chatter. Although they were in their mid-life, when they got together, they became ageless. Nothing could change the way they giggled and the way they nattered.

"Well, I'm going to buy flowers on my way home to-day," Ursula said, suddenly becoming aware of her surroundings. Quietly, she lowered her gaze towards the coffee cup.

"For whom? I hope you haven't got a secret admirer."

"Maybe I do Ulle, who knows?" she said, stirring the coffee as she poured more milk and added half a spoon of sugar.

"No, not at our age, I don't think," said Una.

"It's a deep secret," she said rolling her eyes in mischief. "However, I may tell you one day."

"May?" asked Una apprehensively. "Or, may not. I hope you have a bloody good reason for not wanting to tell us?"

"No reason, not today. That's all, just a bit rushed."

They finished coffee rather hurriedly, picked up their handbags, slung them over their shoulders, and walked out of the café. This was not how they generally parted. They would usually sail out of the café in pure euphoria, laughing, rejoicing, and promising to meet again. Today, however, it was different. Ursula said goodbye, dashing off in the opposite direction, much to both Una's and Ulle's surprise.

"I wonder what she's up to," Ulle muttered,

"Dunno. She really didn't want to share it with us, hey."

"No."

They left it at that.

Ursula walked hastily towards her car. She turned the key in the ignition. Her car headed off north and stopped by a corner shop called, *Brisbane North.* She entered the confectionary and looked at the flowers displayed outside on the pavement. She walked straight past them and picked up a loaf of bread instead as well as a jar of honey. Then, she returned to her car; an impenitent smile appeared on her thick lips. Her car slowly approached the horizon and sped down the road.

151

The next morning, the phone rang. Una let it ring for a while. Then it stopped. She had an apple in her right hand and a pot of beef casserole on the stove. She quickly finished stirring it, and then turned off the stove. The phone rang again. She took a bite from her apple and picked up the phone.

"Hello?"

"Yeah, how's it going?" Ulle asked, clearing her throat.

"Not bad. How're you?"

"Good."

"Any news from our mysterious friend?"

"Not yet. I wonder what she's up to."

"Why not ask her?"

"Oh, look I don't think I could. Why don't you?" Una asked earnestly.

"Well in that case, I shall. I'll ask her to meet up tomorrow."

"That's a good idea. See you tomorrow then."

"Sure, bye for now."

"Bye."

Ulle could not wait to see Ursula the next day. Both Una and Ulle went to the café a little early, bubbling with excitement. The mystery would be solved soon. They would most certainly find out more about the secret admirer today. It was most unnatural for somebody as unromantic as Ursula to buy flowers for anyone. She was so rational that she was almost to the point of being dispassionate. Why? Did she not take a vow that she would remain single because she did not like children?

"No fights over the seats today?" Both Ulle and Una were startled as Ursula crept up from behind.

"Goodness me! You scared me," they both said together turning back.

"And yes, why am I sitting here, in the middle of this horrible crowd?" Una screamed.

"Weird?" Ulle looked aghast at Una then at Ursula.

Ursula was a little bewildered as she took her seat and kept looking at them both. They ordered the usual, but there was an uneasy silence. No one uttered a word. Una signaled Ulle, who cringed back, for words suddenly iced-up. She was clearly afraid of what she might hear. It was unbelievable that Ulle, of all people, could be so coy. This was extraordinary indeed. Friends have swapped personalities, revealing an entirely new side to their characters. So, when they asked nothing, Ursula thought it was up to her to break the ice.

"I guess, you're wondering what secrets I'm keeping from you guys?" she said openly amused, sipping the lukewarm coffee.

"Yes," they both said in agreement.

"Well, I'd like to show you something interesting."

She opened her bag with her left hand and took her mobile phone out with her right. Then, she pressed the buttons on the phone until she came to 'view photos.' Flicking the photos one after another on the mobile, she chose to click on one. When it opened, *walla*, it was a photo of a beautiful child.

"This is who, I buy the flowers for," she said.

"But who is she?" Una asked.

"My little girl."

"Your little girl? Since when? You don't even like children. "

"I never said that."

"Yes you did," Ulle said with eyes wide open.

"I think, I said that I couldn't raise one," a furtive, Mona Lisa smile emerged in the corner of her lips, as she replied nonchalantly. "She's an orphan. I pay for her upkeep."

"Really? How long have you had her?" Una asked.

"Long enough."

"You didn't tell us all this time. Why tell us now?" Ulle harangued.

"Because, I got caught out."

"Do you love her?" Una asked softly.

"I think so."

"Does she like flowers? Perhaps, she would like chocolates better," Ulle suggested.

"Maybe, but I do. I like buying flowers. For others and for me," she paused. "Besides, it's spring. Look around you. Look at the mad colors. We must celebrate, mustn't we?"

It was spring and the flowers did blossom in infinite profusion, but it still didn't explain why it excited Ursula so much.

"Incredible," said Ulle.

"Indeed," said Una.

Ursula said nothing. They left the café a little absorbed. Ursula's mysterious smile lingered on as she walked towards her car. She was pulling their leg of course and they fell for it. Ursula laughed loudly. She got in the car and thought of their curious behavior. How Una forgot about her coyness and Ulle, the vivacious bully, became the *coy mistress.* She sussed them out, but she must keep up her charade and let it go as far as it possibly could. It wouldn't be long before the games began.

A few days went past. Ursula called Ulle one afternoon.

"Ursula? How're you?" Ulle said.

"Look, I won't be able to come tomorrow, or go to the movies."

"Why not?"

"I'm a little busy."

"Busy? Or, is it that you're afraid to spend money?" she asked.

155

"Do you think this is because I don't want to spend money?"

"That's what I think."

"Why, you're a lot thriftier than I ever am."

"Maybe, but you need to chip in more."

"We'll talk later. I must go," said Ursulla.

"Bye.

"Tata."

She thought of the many days, when Ulle had borrowed from her and never really paid her back. She thought of the innumerable occasions that she had not given the exact change for the bigger notes that Ursula had entrusted her with and how there were always shortfalls. She pulled it off every time with her usual loquaciousness, her seeming courage. And now, she was actually accusing her of being miserly. How dare she? However, Ursula said nothing of this. All she said was that she would meet them the next time, that backbiting bitch.

Seething with anger, she hung up and went straight into the shower, thinking how obnoxious this was. In the shower, she thought that she must never disclose the mystery of the child's existence.

Later that afternoon, when Ursula sat at her computer browsing her favorite social site, she pulled the scroll down to see her older messages and comments. The many people she knew and the many she had not known, all those years, all that time, sunk in those intimately emotive or not so emotive posts. People even put their newborn baby's pictures on their profiles, and others wrote when they were married or what they were up to. Did it really matter what they did or did not do? And yet, this was a record of their time in life and how they chose to spend it; the chronicles of an individual, as it were.

It was always possible though, to delete a current post and raise a backdated post up so that happy memories would remain on the page unconditionally. However, people wished the same could be done with life as well. Delete obnoxious posts, bring the happier ones up and keep them there, always at present. Unfortunately, it did not work that way on the timeline of life. No page was immutable. In the end, all was lost in the scroll.

There were no interesting messages or posts today, except for people pouring in from everywhere, debating whether or not *Burqa* should be banned. The futile pursuit people spent their energy on. Ursula's dog looked at her intermittently between sleep and wakefulness.

Una felt a little lonely. None of her friends called of late. She really believed that Ursula might have actually adopted that child, or at least paid for her upkeep, or whatever else she said she did. One afternoon, she sat in her garden pulling out weeds.

While at it, she found something really strange. She picked it up and held it against the sun.

It was an interesting metal that gleamed in the sun's reflection. She thought it might be a thing of considerable value and perhaps an antique piece or something. Anyway, she needed to check it out. She washed the dirt off and thought that she might take it to the jeweler one afternoon. Until then, she hid it in her jewelry box away from everybody's eyes, especially her coffee mates, for who knows what they might do? Ulle might even ask for it. Or, Ursula might say that she was being foolish, taking this good-for-nothing stuff so seriously. She found it interesting. She was going to keep it.

The bell rang. Una ran to the door to open it. She had a parcel. A postman was delivering it. As she signed off the acknowledgement card, Una looked at the sender. It did not look too familiar. She could not wait to open it. But, who was this from? She wondered. It was a book obviously. She thought hard as she opened the parcel. It said, "Ruth Naidoo." Ruth Naidoo? Oh yes, she remembered the author from day care. Ruth was rather pleased with Una when she had gone out of her way to feed her child one day. He was not eating that day.

She copped crap from her fellow workers afterwards, but she did it anyway. Una remembered the awkward moment she had with Ruth as they sat together under the patio of the day care centre and talked about her son's eating problems.

158

Ruth had told her that she was a writer and Una had asked her ignorantly, "Why do you write? Is it because you've got nothing else to do?"

Ruth was shocked, but had not shown it. Instead she had said, "Why don't I send you a copy of my new book? Read it and let me know how it went."

So, this was the book. She leafed through the pages, then put it away thinking that one day she might decide to read it, for Una, who was a high school dropout,t was not much of a reader. When she went into the bathroom later that after-noon to clean the toilet, she saw ants, swarms of them, mounting up the surface of the white wall. It was going to rain and the ants were no doubt out and about. Una resisted the urge to kill them. "Oh, let them get away, while they still can," she said to herself.

Ulle waited in her kitchen when the phone rang. It was from her secret admirer, calling to let her know how pretty she looked as a lollipop lady at the crossing of the children's school, when she bit her nails that morning.

"Where were you?" she asked. "Why didn't you honk me?"

"I didn't want to distract you," he said.

"How're you?"

"Pretty good, and you?"

"Not too bad. We need to catch up. Do you think we could meet?"

"Sure, why not?"

"Do you want to do dinner tonight?"

"Where? Your place or mine?"

"Mine, 'cause I'm cooking."

"I'm already salivating. See you then," he said.

"Sure thing."

They hung up. Ulle went about her chores for the day. She could not decide what to cook. Then, she thought of spaghetti and meat Bolognese. Taking a bath in perfumed soap that evening, she put her best silk on for her admirer. She had met him on the school premises when he had come looking for his poodle. He called the puppy Duke. She had helped him find Duke and ever since became great friends. Now, that friendship was turning into romance. She had told him about her other two coffee mates, Ursula and Una. Tonight, of course, she was going to bitch about them. Although, it was not exactly six 'o'clock yet, he had arrived. Ulle quickly opened the door for him. They kissed on the lips. It was a hot sensuous contact. He put the bottle of wine on the countertop. Ulle steadied herself. Once he released her, he asked her, with a smile,

"Shouldn't we eat first?"

"Yes, by all means."

They lit a couple of candles on the kitchen table and sat down opposite each other. He poured wine into the two glasses.

"How're your friends?" he asked helping himself to salad out of the wooden salad bowl.

"They're good. A bit secretive though."

"How do you mean?"

"Well Ursula has a ward she says; can you believe it? A little girl somewhere that she's been supporting."

"Really? And, she never shared it with you guys before?"

"No. The other day it accidentally slipped out."

"Keeping a secret? But, why? It's a good thing that she's done, I reckon'"

"But, do you know what? I don't even think it's true."

"What do you mean?"

"Well yeah, she said she was going to buy flowers, but I don't even think she did that."

"She lied to you guys?"

"I don't know. That's what I need to find out."

"And, what if she did? How're you going to find out?"

"I got a plan."

"Tell me later," he winked.

As the three of them could not live without each other, they went out yet another day. Reverting to their cloaked selves, they sat once again in their shady corner, the dark place, at the back of the café. Una could not wait to show them the book that she had received from the author friend of hers.

"I've a friend, who is an author," she declared.

"Oh. Since when do you read?" Ulle said. "I've never seen you read ever or even talk about a book in all this time that I've known you."

"I don't think people should be showing off, about their reading habits. If I didn't read, why would my writer friend send me a signed copy of her book?"

"How should we know? Perhaps, you do. Please tell us," said Ursula, being the happy medium as usual.

"Well, I met her at the day care centre when her son wasn't eating. I asked her what she did for a living. She told me that she was a writer. I was overwhelmed, meeting a writer in person. Naturally, I told her how I loved reading. She was really happy about it," Una paused to have a sip of coffee and between the lip and the cup, she said. "She told me that she was going to send me a copy of her latest book. And, that's what arrived yesterday. I love it."

"Aha? What's it about?" asked Ulle but not in earnest, because what if she did read it. She would then have to cope with her own failings, her jealousy. It was better this way.

"Oh, it's a complicated story, just started and finished the first chapter or so."

"Well, tell us once you've finished it," said Ursula, turning to Ulle. "What're you up to these days?

"I wish I could say that I did something noble like you keeping a ward."

"Surely, you've done something interesting?"

"Not really. Last night I dozed off on the couch watching television. The show was so boring, I tell you. And, I didn't get much sleep either."

"Well, Ruth, my writer friend, says she doesn't get much sleep, must be a writer thing."

"Yeah, we all have our crosses to bear, I s'ppose."

Intolerable. Ursula grunted inwardly. "Well I wrote on my butcher's paper yesterday, how to tenderize meat by using a tenderizer."

"Why did you do that for? Was the butchery so quiet yesterday?"

"No, not exactly. I wrote that for a customer. I kind of like writing too. So, I write my stuff in between chopping."

"My writer friend, Ruth, she likes discussing themes with me. It opens up her mind, she says."

"Your writer-friend likes discussing stuff with you?" Ulle laughed sarcastically.

"Yes, she does. She thinks it's really inspirational that she met me."

"I'd say that again," Ursula chuckled.

"By the way, were you able to buy chocolates?" Ulle suddenly confronted Ursula.

"Chocolate? For whom? Myself?"

"No silly. As Una suggested the other day, don't you remember? Take chocolates instead of flowers for your ward, what's her name? Did you tell us her name?"

Quickly thinking of a name, she realized that she had completely forgotten about the chocolate bit. She must be more careful. She nearly gave herself away.

"I call her, Pam."

"Nice name, Pam," Ulle looked at her flustered expression for a while and added. "if she's real, that is."

"Yeah, it is a rather nice name isn't it?" Ursula said confidently, ignoring the skepticism.

"And, when do we see her, if at all? This Pam?"

"Soon," she said, grabbing her bag off the floor.

"Yeah," Ulle said. "When're you going to shout at us again, Ursula?"

"I'll think about it."

What a sucker she had been in the past? Always paid more. Was it her generosity? Or, something else? She couldn't quite figure it out. They paid their shares today and left the cafe in good spirits.

A few days went by and no one heard anything from anyone. Ursula sat at the computer again. When she finished, she put her black skirt on and got ready for work. She thought of her coffee mates, their inane discussions, and realized what a waste of time it had been. However, coffee or no coffee, they must link up once a week at least. She put her mobile and car keys into her bag as she left for the garage door. She stumbled on the side.

Ursula walked a few steps towards the car and turned the key to open the door. The garage door was already open. She reversed the car out into her driveway and parked it. She got out to close the garage door manually. Then, she walked back to the car and sat down in the driver's seat. She thought of the cuts, the lamb chops, and the cubes that she had to do all day. Sniffing her nose, she drove out. She wasn't paying enough attention, and she had not seen the car that had just sped across the roadway just as she was about to make a right turn at the T-intersection. That was close! She inhaled a deep breath.

Her day at the butcher's was uneventfully boring. She stood by her colleagues doing cuts. Looking at the butcher's paper, she found a pen to scribble a few words, writing not about tenderizers, but about how stupid her coffee mates were.

It was now beginning to bother her. She saw through them and into the emptiness of it all. Then, she saw her manager coming. Quietly, she hid the paper inside her apron pocket, but couldn't escape his keen eyes.

He came up to her; towering over her, asked, "What did you just hide from me?"

"It's personal, can't show you."

The manager snickered and disappeared into the cold room behind a huge cow leg. A customer came up to the counter asking for chopped curry meat. She said they did not do those anymore.

"Okay," the customer said. "I'd like you to chop this for me then."

She picked up a leg of lamb from the rack that was displayed with all other cuts and handed it over to her.

"With the bone in if you don't mind, thanks."

"Okay."

She took the leg of lamb, from her hand and walked to the huge, rolling blade machine. The manager in the meantime, came out of the cold room and stood nervously close to her, just at the moment she was about to put the leg through the blade. Suddenly, there was blood everywhere; it came gushing out of her right thumb. The pain! Oh, the unbearable pain! She screamed feeling light-headed and faint. The stupefied customer looked for a while, and then quickly left the scene, mumbling that she might make vegetables that night instead.

Ursula regained her consciousness at the manager's office. Her thumb was bandaged securely around her hand.

"You're lucky that a bit of that thumb was still hanging," he said.

"What happened?"

"You needed to get a reality check, that's what's happened."

"What'd y' mean?"

"I found your butcher's paper. It rolled out of your pocket. Do you want to tell me what's going on that might have caused this injury?"

There was a jug of water on the table. She indicated that she wanted a drink. The manager poured a glass for her and handed it to her. She extended her other hand and took the glass eagerly, averting eye contact. Having a tiny sip of water, she said, barely touching the rim, with her dry lips.   "Won't happen again; I promise."

"Okay, I'll ignore it this time. Next time, I might not be so generous. Keep personal life out of business. Take the day off. You're no good with or without that thumb today."

Ursula came out of the manager's room, with all her co-workers eyeing her from head to toe. She took off her apron, pulled her black vinyl bag from the locker and held it close to her chest. She was okay to drive home for now, but the pain could start any time. She was lucky that she did not lose that thumb altogether.

Overall, she had a masculine get up. Her broad shoulder squared evenly as it joined her short, beefy arms below. Her usual languorous gait facilitated in a way for those arms to hang loosely about when they marched along in slow motion. Her two elbows curved deeply, allowing her forearms to push towards her belly in the front. Quite a sight, especially the way she carried her long dreadlocks, which hung to her shoulders. Today, of course, it was different.

She walked in the strangest, the most inelegant, possible manner as she came out of the shop and proceeded towards the car. She held her bandaged thumb with the other hand, dragging her man feet slowly across as though they were shackled in chains. Her boss could have fired her, but he had not. She got lucky, but she knew the random, mind games this man liked to play with his employees in the name of keeping tabs.

It was not the most difficult thing to do, ask for help, but Una chose not to. One afternoon, a few days after the last meeting with friends, she decided to pay a visit to the jeweler. It was her desire to make earring studs out of the metal object that she had found in her garden. In the pursuit of having a bit of an adventure as well, she decided to go alone. She took the object from her treasure box and put it in her sling handbag, observing that the metal looked like a little gold nugget. She walked out of her house, pulling the door firmly behind her. It self-locked.

It was the breeding season with just a few magpies roaming about. Their aggressiveness was perceived in their behavior, which Una had not noticed. She calmly walked to the bus stop on the Woogeroo Street. There she sat down on the bench comfortably waiting for the bus. A teen aged boy waited too. When she saw the bus, she hailed it and opened her bag to get her purse out.

Catching her unaware, however, a magpie, which was out and about, came towards her. Swooping low, the black and white bird, went straight for her eye and attacked her with all its might. Una, who was not prepared for this strike, lost her composure and became perplexed. She fell off the bench onto the footpath and went into a sudden frenzy. Flapping its wings, the bird soared high and flew over her almost straightaway.

The bus came by in the meantime. It stopped right in front of her. The driver, disembarked quickly, as he saw a woman sitting on the footpath, wailing away. He helped her to rise up on her feet and steered her back to the bench. She bellowed in her high-pitched voice as she told him everything and held on to his arms. When she looked for her bag, it was nowhere to be found. Nonetheless, she held her purse in her hand, although the bag was gone, along with the shiny metal in it.

Soon, she settled down and thanked the driver. Unexpectedly, in the midst of this commotion, a police car was sighted. The driver had sent them a message on his walkie-talkie earlier. The police car was parked in front of the bus and two uniformed officers got out of the car. They walked a few steps towards Una and stood by the bench. When they interrogated her, she told them how a teenager sat beside her at the bus stop and this could very well be his doing. The police took down all the details. Then they asked her if there was anything of value in the bag. She told them about the nugget, reluctantly. The policeman noted it.

She decided not to take the bus that day, but went home instead. She had barely entered the house when there was a knock on her door. Two men stood outside. She quickly opened the door.   "We need to have a chat with you. The police found your bag in the next street. It had nothing in it except, a shiny nugget. We would like to know where you might have found it. These are usually found by gold mines," they said. "A gold mine? In my backyard?" Her eyeballs popped out in amazement.

She opened the door and most graciously let them in. Unable to contain her excitement, she went straight for the phone. This news was too good to pass up. One of her mates must be told. However, the moment she turned around, she found herself in the grips of two strong hands that held her back. She tried to get loose by squirming out of the hold, but could not. In vain, she struggled for a while and then she thought of her legs. Why not use them instead? Quickly, she crouched her knees forward just enough to give her sufficient leeway to raise her legs up to the position of a back kick. This was a task, she was not accustomed to, but for self-preservation, she was compelled to do it. Her feet found their way in between the crotches over the pants into the groins. With two successive kicks, she disabled the hold.

It had not ended there, however, for the second man, who was in the next room rummaging through her things, heard his companion scream a terrible growl. Immediately, he appeared on the scene and made an attempt to go after her while her first attacker doubled over in pain. The hot frying pan, which was still on the nearby stove, unpredictably came to her rescue. She grabbed it in one sway of her arm straight off, and 'bang' and then another 'bang.' Again and again, Una whacked on both their heads and called for help, "Someone, please help!"

The two thugs fell down on her kitchen floor. A neighbor who heard her through the open door, called the police. The police came again and arrested the men. It turned out that an entire gang was racketing around the place for a while. This gang targeted only single occupants on this street for the convenience of mugging. It was not hard to find her. When police were taking notes on the street, they kept her under close vigilance. The rest was easy. All they did was follow her home.

Being in the center of this drama, Una now proudly spread the word around how she became a part of this and because of her nugget the scammers were found today and arrested.

However, the contribution of the magpie did not go unrewarded either. In its own way, it was just as important a participant as Una herself. The tale of the humble nugget made Una the talk of the town. She was in the community newspapers, also in the local news briefly, and her picture even appeared in leaflets, with a huge magpie sitting on her shoulder with the heading: '*The Accidental Hero.*' She endlessly talked about it and bragged about it until her mates told her to just shut up about it.

They had gone out to have coffee one afternoon, after Ursula started feeling better. She did not share her incident with anyone. She did not want to give them the pleasure. Since then, the bandage was taken off, but there was a scar, which she covered with a ring in the thumb. That was what she wished to do from now on.

Ursula tried to avoid any discussion about her ward lately. Every time the subject matter came up, the only thing that she ever said was, 'She's not too well,' and averted the topic.

Of all her friends, only Una had a small victory that she could boldly claim as hers. This made Ursula feel slightly uncomfortable. She suspected that the story about her ward might not have gone down too well.

"Let's order," said Ulle looking at Ursula, while Una shifted uneasily in her chair. They continued to sit in the dark corner, although it was proven beyond any shadow of a doubt that Una's coyness was just a pretense to seek a bit of attention, which she finally got. When Ursula did not say anything about paying, Ulle gave Una an edgy look. After an awkward moment, she conceded.

"Well, alright, I'll shout you guys today."

"Please do."

Ursula couldn't ignore the palpable anxiety in their voice when she said that she would pay for the coffee. It felt as though their coffee meeting would somehow fall apart if she did not shout them today. They had grown to depend on it.

The coffee arrived, Ursula took a sip from it, but that nagging suspicion did not give her a moment's peace. She stole a look at Ulle, her fingers fiddling around the edge of the little cup holder tensely and in a tight grip.

"What's new in your life, Ulle?"

Ursula asked suddenly, thinking that this might suppress the unwarranted suspicion that was being raised in their minds.

"Oh, the usual. Why do you ask?"

"Well you haven't really said anything exciting, that you might've done, lately?"

Ulle's left eye started to twitch suddenly as she felt the pang of a nervous attack. She thought of her boyfriend, who might just be using her. She thought how he might leave her for another woman. Awful! How awful! Ursula kept looking at her seemingly calm face.

"Well don't just twiddle your thumbs all day; do something with your life. How long do you think that you can be a lollipop lady?"

The wind was suddenly knocked out of her sails. The bully kept quiet and Una looked at both of them out of the corner of her eye.

"Am I missing something?"

"No," both of them said together.

"Okay." Una said looking at them awkwardly.

"And, how's Ruth?"

They were onto her now.

"Who?"

They were both quiet. Una got up as the table tweaked shakily and said that she needed to go.

"Yeah, me too," said Ursula.

She paid for the coffee. They left the café in a slightly offbeat mood.

A few days passed, there were no contacts. If only Ulle could get her boyfriend to give her a wedding ring that she could flaunt, that would be worthwhile. Then, she could also have something to brag about as much as Ursula and Una. At the school crossing one day, when Ulle was working, she received an sms. It was from her boyfriend, Michael. He was letting her know that their meeting for that evening was off.

Ulle frowned thinking that something was not right. He had not called her all this time. Today's meeting was Ulle's initiative. Was he trying to squirm out of it? She sent him an sms asking him for a reason, to which he only said, he would tell her later. 'He's calling it quits, I'm sure of it. I think he's cheating on me,' she said to herself. She decided to go to his house after she finished here. What would she say to her friends, if Michael decided to break up now? She had the most horrible pain in her chest followed by shortness of breath, but she would live.

Una called Ursula, when she had not heard from either of them for a while.

"Hey, how's it going?"

"Good," said Ursula as she was making a ham and lettuce sandwich.

"Have you heard from Ulle?"

"No, have you?"

"Not really."

"I wonder what's up. She's usually not this quiet."

"No, why don't you give her a call?" Ursula suggested.

"Yeah, I might do that actually. I'll call her now after I hang up with you."

"Sure. Talk to you later. Have to run."

"Okay. Bye then."

"Bye."

Una called Ulle, but the phone rang out. "She's never in these days, is she? Where could she have gone? I'll try later on."

She opened the fridge, took out cold potato and egg salad; as she was just about to sit down in her cozy cocoon to have dinner and watch television, her phone rang. The halogen lamp was turned on in the room, enhancing its coziness with a nice settee and a coffee table. Over a thick woolen rug, the TV sat opposite the sofa on a TV stand. There were some cookbooks on the coffee table, which enlightened her once in a while, exposing her to the world of print. She put down the salad bowl and went to pick up the phone. It was Ulle.

"Did you try to call me?"

"How did you know?"

"Your number was on call waiting. I was on another call. And, guess what?

"What?"

"Michael proposed. He gave me a diamond ring."

"Who on earth is Michael? You never told us about him?"

"No, we'd only just met. I wanted to tell you but wasn't sure, which way the relationship was heading. Well, he's finally proposed."

"This calls for celebration. When can we meet?"

"Why not this Friday? I'll tell Ursula right now. Or, did you?"

"I'll tell her. I'll call her now."

"We'll see you soon.

"See ya."

Now, this was news. Una could hardly eat her salad. Not that she was exactly ecstatic, but thinking that she too might meet someone, and settle down one day. This was good, but too good to be true. Suspicion obviously came naturally to her, as she had a few odd lies of her own. That evening when she did dishes, suds flowed over the sink a little. She bent down to wipe them off the floor.

The scalding frying pan was still on the stove since that evening when she had used it to fry the French toast for tea. She grabbed its handle and put it down in the sink full of soapy water to cool it down. It did not hiss and no black smoke came off it. She hated the black smoke, for it always stifled her. She looked at the grimy wipe and threw it away in the piled up garbage bin. Then, she took the garbage out.

A sudden lightening flashed across the dark sky as she held up the lid with one hand and put the garbage into the bin with the other. The brooding clouds had darkened the full yellow moon in a mud-spattered clad. The rolling sound of the thunder startled her so much that she ran impulsively inside. She went into the bathroom to wash her hands quickly then to brush her teeth. Her fingers shook as she changed into her pajamas. She thought of Ulle and minutes later, she turned off the lights. Curling up in bed, she closed her eyes, still feeling jittery and held her hands close to her chest in a tight fist. No sooner had the storm started, than the winds began to lash out at the branches.

There was huge crackling noise right outside her window. The sounds of the hail had not stopped on the tiled roof, until after midnight, but Una was fast asleep. It had cooled down considerably the next morning. She woke up, drew the curtains, and let the bright sunlight stream through the glass window.

"Now, how can you be so sure?" Ursula asked Una. "I mean, honestly, who in his right mind would propose to Ulle?"

"I don't know. I guess only Ulle can tell us, but I can't say that I disbelieved her. She sounded so confident,"

"Wouldn't you? If you had to convince people of somethin' pretty bad? But, then you would believe her, wouldn't you? 'Cause you'd believe anythin' and everythin.' If Ulle were here, she wouldn't exactly call you kind, no offence, but she might call you gullible."

"She would have, I s'ppose."

Una's deceptiveness was perceptible to Ursula. However, she was preoccupied with something even more insidious. Una saw a strange kind of jealousy in her that she had not seen before. "Is it possible though that Ursula might be jealous?" The little voice said in her mind. They waited for Ulle impatiently at their regular spot that afternoon.

Ulle was not usually late; on the contrary, she was always early. What could possibly have kept her today, the day of the celebration? Between now and the last call, neither of them spoke to each other. To pass the time, they talked casually about the storm, how ferocious it was, and how it ravaged cars and killed people.

179

After Ulle had hung up with Una the night before, she went straight into the shower. She had also heard the grumblings of the thunder that night, the fricative *"sh"* of the wind's sound reverberating through the elongated leaves of the lofty trees. The gum tree in her backyard took most of the beating, but the roof of her cottage took some too as the hail fell incessantly on. Ulle was just as frightened. She thought her tiny weatherboard cottage might not be strong enough to weather the storm and it would blow away at the huff and the puff of three. The mighty Ulle had not called Ursula; instead, she hid under the blanket until she fell asleep. However, just before falling asleep, she had sat on the edge of her high bed with the soft mattress and opened one of the drawers of her bedside table. She took a ring box out. Considering the box on her lap, she opened it gently with her small, chubby fingers. Then, she pulled the ring out off the casket groove. With a touch of malicious joy in the corner of her lips, she sat looking at the shiny, white mounted stone.

The next day, she called her first thing in the morning, just before heading off for work. Ursula's reaction was strangely apathetic. "Did she say she was getting married? How on earth could she live with a man?" She tried to understand. But, she had congratulated Ulle and agreed to meet her on the appointed day.

The friends waited at the coffee club, when she finally arrived. She looked like a smiling bride already. They stared at her in amazement. She looked calm, collected, and confident.

She uttered a "Hi," pulled out a chair, and sat down with a thump. Placing the ring finger conspicuously on the table, she pushed the chair all the way up.

"You've done it," said Una.

"Yes, I managed to bag this one *alright*."

"Where did you meet him?" Ursula asked deviously.

Aware of the searching looks, coming from both, she told them about their meeting. "They don't believe me, do they?" She thought warily, taking a sharp breath.

"So, when's the wedding?" Una asked curiously.

"Dunno know, yet," she pouted her lips and shrugged.

Ursula found this whole affair quite intriguing for she doubted the wedding. She seriously wondered whether or not there was a proposal in the first place. Bending her head down, she tried to take a closer look at the ring, to check if it was a fake stone. Ulle jerked and stood up. With a head-turning resounding noise, the chair fell. Her mates jumped too, not sure what had happened. Ulle turned around, walked straight out of the café, and deserted them. Both followed her, stunned as they braced themselves for the worst.

"What did we do?" Una cried.

"Nothing," Ulle said.

"Nothin'? Surely, somethin' happened," said Ursula.

"Leave me alone."

They stood back at that. They let her go. Una and Ursula exchanged stoned looks. Both shrugged together, making their way to the car park. They suddenly realized that it was the charade that kept them going. Without it they felt lonely and empty. It was a case of embracing the 'necessary evil,' the loss of which was terrifying.

"I'll call you," she said.

'I'll call you too."

Ursula drove away as Una walked slowly towards the bus stop. The panic button was triggered to which Ulle showed her true colors. The bully had succumbed to her own vulnerability and brought an end to this game, the game of constant upstaging and subversion. It was quite a convincing charade otherwise, but for those sporadic moments that educed elemental fears exposed and compromised it. When the mask came off, no one stood her ground. They *all* did a runner, a reflex action shared in the butcher's paper as an innate endowment, although their fingerprints were different as the night was from the day.

Melinda Tarcon

I am Melinda.
I am a 44 year old,
wife, mother, daughter, sister and friend.

I worship Jesus.
While my love for Him is so very imperfect,
His love for me is completely perfect.

I drink a lot of coffee.
Like, *A LOT*!

I like to eat delicious food.
Like cake,
and potato chips,
and pop-corn loaded with butter,
and KFC,
and
pretty much all the stuff that is bad for you.
And,
I don't even care.

I sing,
I like to sing.

I laugh,
too loud,
and for too long.
Also,
I snort when I laugh.
I hate that.

I write.
I am a writer.
Not a superbly skilled writer,
but,
people seem to like what I write.

I love.
I love people.
(And cats.)

Also,
wine.

A River For Jordan - http://melindatarcon.blogspot.ca/2016/08/a-river-for-jordan.html
I Write. I Am A Writer -
http://melindatarcon.blogspot.ca/2016/08/i-write-i-am-writer.html

The Great Iced-Coffee Catastrophe

It had been an absolutely wonderful day.

My husband and I had attended our daughter's final Region B Swim Meet.

This was a big deal.

We were expectantly hoping for a fourth place finish in her best race.

She miraculously pulled off third.

A bronze medal!

Never had a medal been celebrated more!

We were exultant!

There was no parent in Rio more excited than me or my husband!

We were both so proud of her!

We were *so* happy!

We were so *in love*!

As we pulled out on to the main road out of St. Albert, we were discussing where we wanted to stop to grab a bite to eat.

Jason and I were thinking iced-coffee would be pretty much perfect for the road home.

My daughter wanted a burger and ice-cream.

And let me tell you, you guys.

This is where the problem started.

Jason informed me that I was the one responsible to pick the spot to stop.

Look.

I don't like making decisions.

I find it stressful.

It's too *hard*!

What if pick something that no one likes?

What if I make the wrong decision?

I *HATE* making the wrong decision.

"But, make sure you give me enough warning to turn." he said.

Lord help me.

"And make sure the turn off is wide enough for the trailer."

Panic.

Ok, I thought.

I can do this.

I can **do** this!

This is not a big deal.

Just scan ahead and look for a great place.

I frantically searched for this perfect place that would cover all the required criteria...

Iced-coffees for me and Jay.

A burger and ice-cream for the girl.

A wide enough place to turn for the trailer.

And absolutely **not** last minute.

And then he says, "Actually, I think there's a Starbucks and a DQ up by the Costco.

Glory and Hallelujah!

I am saved!

He knows where to turn well in advance.

There is more than enough room for the trailer.

We will all get exactly what we want!

Thank you Jesus!

We pull in, and people???

Life is good.

The crisis has been averted.

And then he says,

"How about I go with the girl and get her burger, and you go to Starbucks and and get us our iced-coffees?"

Ok.

Ok.

I very quickly debate this idea.

Do I go get the iced-coffees and risk getting the wrong thing?

Or do I go with the girl and be put through the trauma of *that* ordering experience?

Look, people.

Both of these decisions are *hard*.

There is no win for me here.

If I choose the girl.......

Half the time I cannot understand a word my daughter says.

She mumbles.

Like, she seriously mumbles!

"Pardon me?" I ask.

She proceeds to mumble some more.

I start to feel real fear now, because I KNOW there is the potential for her to lose her ever-lovin' mind.

She is 14 and scary.

"Um, ah...... *Pardon me*?"

"Oh, just **FORGET IT!** You never listen to anything I say, anyway!"

I am afraid of her.

And if I choose my man.......

The problem here is,

We don't often get iced-coffees from Starbucks.

Hot coffees, yes.

So, I can choose a hot coffee that I know he will like.

But, iced-coffees, not so much.

I would be going in blind.

I would have to choose on my own.

It would be a great gamble.

He is awfully particular about what he likes.

I can usually figure out something.

But, not **always.**

I was afraid.

But, I was afraid to go with the girl, too.

I chose.

Wrongly.

I look at my husband, and with a last grasp at hope, I ask if he knows what he would like.

"You know what I like. Just pick me something."

I should have changed my decision right here, people.

I wish I would have.

But, I didn't.

"I can do this." I thought. "How hard can it be?"

Stupid, stupid girl.

I bravely walk to the Starbucks, open the door, walk up to the counter, and proceed to completely fall apart.

"What can I get for you today?"

Happy, cheery voice.

"Um......ah.........well.......... I need iced-coffees."

"Ok. What kind would you like?"

Happy cheery voice.

"Um, well, I don't really know. What's good?"

I am an idiot.

"Well, we have a nice coconut mocha iced-coffee."

Still the happy, cheery voice, but I'm pretty sure she thinks I am an idiot.

"Well, I'm not sure if he likes coconut. I can't remember."

Now I KNOW she thinks I'm an idiot.

"Just gimme me a minute.........."

"Sure!"

Idiot.

"Um, ok. Ok. I will get a.........um...........I will get a............

Gimme a caramel macchiato iced-coffee!"

Praise the Lord! I made a choice for him!

"What size?"

Apparently this hell was not yet over.

"Well, what are the sizes again? Like, I mean, what do they look like? You know, how big?"

Could the ground just swallow me up right now?!? I think I may have just died.

"Well, this is the short, this is the tall........."

She proceeds to show me.

"Medium. I'll take the medium."

"So, the tall?"

She is totally confused.

Me too, girl. Me too.

"Yeah, the medium........ah, tall."

Loser.

"Is that everything?"

I really want you to leave the store. You are freaking me out.

"Well, no. I would like the coconut one, too."

Painless.

"What size?"

Please know what size you want.

"Tall."

I am a rock star!

"Ok. That will be $10.something please."

Thanks heavens she is done!

"Okee dokee!"

I'm super happy now because the choice is made and I'm feeling pretty confident about it.

"I'm just going to go pee and then come back to grab the iced-coffees, ok?"

"Sure."

Girl, you just go do your thing so that I can talk about you behind your back to my co-worker here, because never in my life have I ever had a bigger idiot come to my till.

I go do my thing.

I come back to get my iced-coffees.

She puts the first one up.

It's not blended.

Crap.

I begin to panic again.

I don't know what to do, now.

I'm fairly certain that Jason is expecting a blended iced-coffee.

But, this is most certainly *not* a blended iced-coffee.

I don't think he will be pleased with this.

This is pretty much the same thing as me asking him to bring KFC for me,

and he shows up with pizza.

I would murder him for a mistake like that.

I'm not even kidding.

But, I begin to rationalize.

191

He said he wanted an iced-coffee.

So, you know, I ordered an iced-coffee.

That blended stuff is not the same thing.

That blended stuff is...................I begin to scan the menu board again.

Frappucino!

That blended stuff is frappucino!

It has it's very own category on the menu board.

It is not the same thing as an iced-coffee!

And he asked me for an iced-coffee, not a frappucino.

This is fine.

This will be fine, I lie to myself.

But, on the inside though, my belly is turning to jello.

I KNOW this will not be fine.

I KNOW he expects an iced-coffee to be blended.

I KNOW what he likes.

What he thinks.

It's just that I forgot that I needed to order it blended.

I forgot because I was in a panic about what to order him in the first place.

So, really, this is his own stupid fault.

Well, maybe this is what he actually wanted, I think.

I crossed my fingers. Figuratively speaking.

She puts the second iced-coffee up on the counter.

I grab them both,

say an enthusiastic thank you to the barista,

put straws in them,

and proceed to walk out the door.

I can feel the barista rolling her eyes at me as I leave..........

I walk to the truck.

They are in there waiting.

Is he staring at the iced-coffees???

He is!

He is staring at the iced-coffees!!!

He knows, already!

He knows they are not blended!

Blast!

I open the door.

I hand him his iced-coffee,

and proceed to climb in the passenger seat and close the door.

He puts the truck in gear and begins to pull out of the parking lot.

He has not said a word.

I'm saved! I think.

"These are not blended."

I die inside.

"I know." I reply with fake confidence. "Iced-coffees are generally not blended."

"But, I like my iced-coffees blended."

"Well, Jason, we talked about getting iced-coffees, so that's what I got."

My voice is slightly elevated.

"But, you know I like them blended. I ALWAYS get them blended."

"Well, you didn't ask for a blended iced-coffee! You asked for an iced-coffee! So I ordered you an iced-coffee! If you wanted a blended iced-coffee you should have asked for a blended iced-coffee, but you didn't so I got you an iced-coffee!"

If I'm going down, I'm going down fighting, folks!

"It's like you don't even know me!"

"What?!? Did you just say that to me?!? How can you even say that to me?!? Of course I know you! I order you the right stuff all the time! How many times have we ordered coffee and I remind you that you like your coffee extra hot? Which *you* always seem to forget to order! See? I do know you! I do so! It's very hurtful that you would say this kind of stuff to me since we both know it's not true! I know you. And you darn well know I know you!"

I may have gone a bit overboard here.

"But I always get my iced-coffees blended. I just wish you would have remembered that."

Reasonable expectation.

"Well, look! I just ordered what you said you wanted, ok?!? Stop complaining and just drink it!"

I was hanging on tightly to my righteous indignation.

Silence.

I think I may have won.

"You ordered it non-fat, right?"

I said a curse word in my head.

I will tell you this straight up.

If there is anything I know about my husband, I **know** he always orders **everything** non-fat.

Like, **everything.**

I know this.

But, in my ordering panic, I simply forgot.

I simply forgot to order his caramel macchiato iced-coffee with non-fat milk.

I am a disgrace to wives everywhere.

He is waiting for an answer.

"Yes."

I lied.

I am a big, fat liar.

I am a terrible person.

I am a terrible wife.

I am going straight to hell for lying to my husband.

I can't do this.

I feel sick.

I think I'm going to be sick.

I CANNOT lie to my husband.

"Wait. Actually, I think I forgot to order it non-fat."

Lord, forgive me for lying to my husband.

I will never, ever do that again.

I honestly couldn't live with myself if I did.

"I ALWAYS ORDER NON-FAT!!!"

"Look! I know! But I forgot! Ok??? I forgot! I was in such a panic about what to order you, that I just forgot to order your iced-coffee non-fat, ok? You have no idea how difficult it is to order you something when you don't tell me what you want! I never seem to order the right thing! It stresses me out! Next time you go and order for the both of us because I *never* complain about what you get me, *ever*! I just graciously accept what you order me and drink it with love in my heart! *I never complain!*"

(Except for two weeks ago, on our 20th anniversary when you went out and got me balloons because you actually know me, and you know I like balloons better than flowers, weird as that is, and you bring them into the house with such love for me saying 'Happy Anniversary!' and I ask you why you got green and ivory balloons instead of green and peach balloons. Yeah, except for that *one* time.)

There is a little more arguing back and forth.

I don't even remember what was said.

Then, my daughter starts laughing at us from the back seat.

"You guys are like an old married couple!"

I am knocked off my pedestal.

"Well, we *are* old." I say quietly.

We are quiet.

I exchange my coconut iced-coffee, because it is a healthier option, with Jason's full-fat iced-coffee.

We both drink our iced-coffees.

He puts his hand on my leg.

All is well.

We are in love again.

Five and a half hours later, we are lying in bed.

"I can't sleep." He says. "You should have got me a decaf."

Fire truck.

G. Allen Cook

G. Allen Cook lives with his wife and son in Northeast Arkansas. He is a playwright, composer, and short story writer. To find more info on his work, please visit www.gallencook.com. You can also find him on Twitter as @TrebleWriter. G. Allen is a regular contributor to "Robbed of Sleep," a fine horror anthology, and makes his humor anthology debut in this publication.

No Easy Trick

Life's not all beer and skittles when your name is Hugo Shmuntz. Doesn't look good on business cards—looks worse on a nameplate. But one does the best one can.

When one's best, however, leaves one without employment, bereft of social opportunity, and an ex-wife who makes a tapeworm seem sexually appealing, one is left with few choices.

I've spent three days mulling said choices, all from the comfort of a single chair left to me under the terms of the divorce. Oh, and I've a mattress crumpled in the floor of what once was the dining room—the extent of my worldly possessions.

Three days. No sleep, drink, food of significant nourishment in that time. A bath would be heaven, but the tapeworm took all the towels, and I don't feel like capering about in the nude to dry myself, even in bitter temperatures with no central heat.

And I'm still Hugo Shmuntz. Where's the justice in that?

* * *

I fumble the bottle top open, spilling green pills into the carpeting. Scooping them up, I pop a dozen or more into my mouth, knock them back with a swallow of beer, and repeat the process. I'm not sure what I'm taking—the bottle's label is worn to a smudge—but its contents are sure to do the trick. I slump in my chair, waiting for the world to fade to black.

It doesn't happen.

An hour later, I'm left to wonder what went wrong. Running my hand across the floor, I come across a pill I'd missed, pick it up, turn it over to see a single capital letter imprinted upon it.

I'd tried to overdose on vitamin E.

Son of a bitch.

* * *

Searching through a disorganized medicine cabinet, I come across a razor blade...ancient and rusted, unused for God knows how long. I sit in the bathtub—I'm told that's how it's done—and roll up a sleeve. The vein is hard to see, at first, but pumping my fist and flexing my arm brings it closer to the surface of the skin.

200

Taking a breath and holding it, I press the razor against the bluest part of the artery and slice with great force and as quickly as possible.

My arm remains intact.

I try it again, but the razor is dull and bends like rubber. Taking a closer look, I discover it is rubber—a leftover gag gift from some long ago Christmas party.

"Amuse your friends" is says on one side.

We are not fucking amused.

***

I turn the oven knob to its highest setting. Settling myself on the narrow floor of the kitchenette, I open the stove door and breathe deep of the deadly gas. For a moment, it seems a wave of dizziness washes over me, but I realize it's due to my heavy breathing bringing on hyperventilation. The gas has no detectable effect.

Becoming impatient, I shove my head into the oven itself. It's as cold inside as it is without. And then I remember: They'd shut my gas off days ago.

I'm trying to asphyxiate myself on pure air.

I hang my head in desperation, banging it on the oven's rim. A small drip of blood splashes the range top. It's as close to doing myself in as I've come all night.

***

Putting on my coat, I wander into the frigid night. Not

far from my apartment winds a busy rail line—I make for it and drape myself across the tracks. No way to cock this up, I tell myself as the whoop of an approaching train splits the otherwise silent night.

The metal lines vibrate with the engine's oncoming power. I close my eyes and spread myself out as to ensure complete dismemberment.

The train rounds a corner and careens toward me. I see the engine's light even through closed lids. It comes, bringing a merciful end to a pitiful life.

It comes! It comes! It—

—splits along another line, taking it north of my sprawled body. I sit up and watch it pass, cursing the good luck that suddenly decides to afflict me.

I lob every oath I know at the waning caboose, adding a few new ones made up on the spot. Picking myself up, I trudge down the line, but there are no more trains tonight.

Tramping my way back toward my apartment, I come across a gang of youths, each of them looking dangerous alone, the group appearing downright lethal.

Here's my chance, I tell myself.

I approach the teenagers and cough to make known my presence. They turn on me, sneering.

"What have we here?" says one.

"Looks a little lost, he does," says another.

"Maybe we ought to teach him not to be out past his bedtime," says a third.

"Perhaps you ought to do just that," I reply. "In fact, before you begin, you each should know that I fornicated with your mothers, and it was good. Or bad. Whichever makes you angriest."

A sense of confusion falls among them. One with a bright blue mohawk—obviously the leader—steps toward me. "What did you say?" he rumbles.

"Um," I say, somewhat regretting my actions. "Well, I said that I...I slept with...that is to say, had...er, carnal relations with...each of your...um...mothers."

A disconcerting silence. A dozen pair of eyes goggle at me in disbelief. Blue Mohawk puts a hard hand on my shoulder.

"Do you know what we are?" he asks.

Heart thumping in my chest, I say, "A menace to society?"

"We're orphans," he replies. "We've just aged out of the children's home. Do you know what that makes you?"

I gulp. "N-N-No. What?"

Blue Mohawk throws both arms around me, as does the entirety of the group. "Father! At last, you've found us!"

"Father?" I cried. "No, you don't understand!"

"If you had carnal relations with our mother," say one of the boys, "that makes you our father!"

203

"At last, lads," says Blue Mohawk. "A parent to take us in!"

***

How I outran them and barricaded myself in my apartment, I'll never know. They gave quite the chase, calling me "father" and "daddy" all the way, but I lost them and made the final sprint home.

It becomes obvious to me that I lack the proper skills to do this the easy way. But one procedure remains—the tried and true method—and so I resolve myself to the painful termination I would've rather avoided.

Pulling my belt from around my waist, I crawl atop the kitchenette's counter, loop the belt over a beam supporting a single row of cabinets, and twine and buckle it beneath my chin. I dread the thought of mucking things up, so I make sure the belt is tightly lashed.

On the count of three, then, I'll step off.

One.

Two.

Three.

***

Knocking on the door, followed by a feminine voice.

"Hugo? Are you there? I've come back. I'm ready to try our relationship again. Hugo?

"Hugo?"

204

Peter Marino

Peter Marino is an English professor at SUNY Adirondack. His novels for young adults *Doughboy* and *Magic and Misery*, were both nominated for YALSA's Best Books for Young Adults. *Magic and Misery* made *Booklist's* Top 10 Fiction for Youth and the ALA Round Table's Rainbow Books Bibliography.

See his work at http://www.petermarinowriter.com/ and http://aquabelll.wixsite.com/yourrightimdead

My Stepfather, The Hawk
A Children's Story with an Appalling Moral

My father had been ripped from my life when I was young, killed leading a cow from our barn on West 89th Street in Manhattan to our pasture along Riverside Drive. Although I was too young to remember it, that terrible day we had lost a father, a husband, and our urban-agricultural zoning permit.

After my real dad died, Mother and I moved to a farm in the country. Since it was just me and Mother, I grew up as the man of the house. Occasionally, an uncle or older cousin would visit us to make sure the farm was running smoothly and that Mother wasn't making me help her in the kitchen or wear a dress, but mainly I did everything: the plowing, the haying, the bookkeeping, and the leading of cows to pasture.

I was nine years old when Mother found a wounded hawk near the creekbank. Someone had shot him in the left wing with a rifle, leaving him to die a slow death. Mother brought him home and kept him in the barn; every day she brought him fresh mice and frogs which she hunted herself. Eventually the hawk grew stronger. He could soon fly again, but his nose-dives often ended in near-crashes. Somehow, he always pulled up just before impact. He would be tired afterward and have to rest.

He was a beautiful hawk, having one large rounded wing and a majestic tail. (Mother and I learned to look the other way when his mangled wing was revealed.) He wasn't colorful, but he was to color my life more than anyone else ever would.

I didn't think much about the hawk becoming a part of our lives at first. I figured he would be gone as soon as he got well, so I really never considered that he and Mother would start getting close. To tell the truth, I really didn't notice that Mother was spending more and more time in the barn— sometimes all day—until it was too late.

Then the hawk began spending time in our house. I didn't particularly like the way he would look at me with his beady suspicious eyes and screech, "Haven't I seen you some place before? Do you own a gun?" But I knew he was probably suspicious of everyone because of his accident. At other times he was perfectly pleasant. He would eat dinner with us and tell me stories of his days as a fearsome hunter. Sometimes a look of unutterable sadness would film over his eyes, as if he were acknowledging that those days were gone for good.

It felt almost okay to have another guy around the house, or at least a male of some species. Mother soon confided that she was falling in love with the hawk, and that she was very afraid. *Love* was a word seldom used in our home— Mother was frightened of love since Father died and she often told me as much. She said that if she never loved again she would never be hurt again. In fact, when she used to tuck me in at night she'd say, "Good night, Billy. I like you. I like you very much."

But the hawk, she now explained, was changing her mind about all that. I thought.

Mother sounded like a school girl with a first crush, although I wasn't sure because I had never met a girl. As Mother and the hawk became more serious romantically, I began to feel a twinge of apprehension. Did Mother really love the hawk and only like me? Was the hawk taking my place as head of the family? Would we have to keep eating those vile meals forever? The first few nights the hawk ate dinner with us, Mother made human food like hamburger or steak, knowing that the hawk was a carnivore. But he ignored her efforts and so she gradually developed a flourish for old-fashioned country predator cooking, Rodent Kidney Pie and Vermin Bake, and the hawk's favorite, Pigs in a Blanket, which was really field mice in a mound of mud. The worst part was that I was sent to catch the food, a task I came to resent.

"You look like you're losing some weight there, son," the hawk said to me one day.

"What do you mean *son*?" I challenged.

Mother interceded. "Billy, dear. You know how much I like you. Well, I wanted you to be the first to know." She looked at the hawk perched on her arm, then giggled. "I guess I mean the third to know. The hawk and I are getting married!"

I don't mean to be melodramatic, but finding out that your mother is getting married again after you've been the head of the household for so long is as shocking as discovering there's no Easter Bunny. At least she wasn't marrying a rabbit.

I tried to hate Mother and the hawk from that day on, but I really couldn't. It was as if the three of us had become a family in a strange way. And I was unwillingly drawn to the notion of being taken care of, of having two parents, of being just a kid. I tried to fight it, but it felt okay.

That is, until their wedding day, when it became clear that I was no longer an equal in the family. I'll never forget the night of the wedding. After the guests had gone back to their homes and dens and lairs, Mother and the hawk said goodnight to me, then went into Mother's room together. This confused me. I felt completely left out. I knocked on the bedroom door, then opened it and stuck my head in sheepishly.

"May I come in with you tonight, Mother? The three of us can stay up and tell stories about hunting."

The hawk let out a guffaw and Mother giggled.

"Not tonight, Billy," the hawk said, still chuckling. Then he continued, patronizingly, "After two people get married, they want to be alone that first night. Just the two of them. I'll explain it to you sometime, but not now."

I was crushed. I closed the door but sat there on the hall floor weeping softly. I thought my heart would just about break in two pieces. It seemed I had been there whimpering an hour when suddenly the door whizzed open and the hawk flew out, enraged. With his beak he grabbed me by the neck of my pajamas and transported me through the air to my room. He flew at such a steep angle that I was sure we would both plunge down the stairs, but once again he managed to keep from crashing. He dropped me on my bed, swatted my rear with his good wing, and screeched, "All that time I thought it was your mother moaning, and it was you! Now get in your bed and don't get up again!" He flew out, slamming the door behind him.

At first I was so shocked I couldn't breathe. The shock slowly gave way to anger. So that was how it was going to be! Thrown out of my own mother's bedroom in my own house.

And by a stranger! And he was going to explain it all to me later, was he? We'd just see about that. The nerve of that hawk, giving me orders as if I were just a little kid.

As it turned out, that particular incident foreshadowed the really big fight two weeks later that was to change my life. The hawk, now in the habit of telling me what to do around the house and on the farm, woke me up earlier and earlier each morning to catch small creatures for his breakfast.

One morning while Mother was still asleep and starvation was gnawing at my temperament, I was plain fed up. I went to the swamp as usual, but after a half-hearted and resentful attempt returned with only a tadpole that I had found already dead. The hawk eyed it contemptuously and said, "You can do better than that, my boy. Go see if you can't catch me something more substantial. Hurry now."

I threw the tadpole on the floor and yelled, "I'm not your boy! And you can't tell me what to do!"

The hawk flew at me with breakneck speed.

"Screech! Screech!" He jabbed me with his powerful hooked bill and seized me by the seat of the pants with his talons. He flew insanely around the kitchen with me captive, then dropped me face first on the kitchen table.

"You can't do that!" I howled as I climbed down. "You're not the man of the house, I am!"

"I'll rip your head off and spit in your neck," he screamed in his horrible voice and flew at me for another attack. I ran for my life for the kitchen door and didn't look back, just yanked the door open enough to get out, then slammed it as hard as I could.

I ran away from the house, sobbing, toward the creekbank where Mother had first found the hawk.

"I wish she had never found him!" I cried as if the creek could hear me. "I wish he was dead! I wish Mother was dead! I wish we were all dead!" I crumbled on the bank and cried myself into a dead sleep.

****

I don't know how long I slept before I felt Mother gently shaking my shoulder. I sat up abruptly, trying to brace myself for the bad news I sensed she had.

"Billy," she said evenly, "it's the hawk. He's dead."

My eyes must have been as wide as the hawk's good wing. I couldn't believe it. As angry as I was at him, I had never wanted him dead.

"Was it his wound?" I asked. "I thought he was getting better."

"Somehow his head got slammed in the kitchen door."

I could barely make the walk home. A squeezing sensation in my chest made me feel like my body was collapsing from the inside. I'm glad Mother interpreted this as grief rather than guilt. I couldn't confess to her. I couldn't admit that I was the one who had ended her long-sought happiness.

When we got home, two veterinary EMTs were taking the hawk out on a stretcher. There was a bloody sheet over him. I asked them to wait a second before putting him in the ambulance. I lowered the sheet and gasped. His head was gone. Sticking out of his neck was a banana, which one of the EMTs must have inserted as a joke. I pulled the banana out and threw it on the ground. Both of the men looked away, ashamed. I turned back to the body and stared at it for a long, hard time, then covered it with the sheet again. Silently, respectfully now, they took him away.

The rest of that agonizing night I had only one thought to console me: At least I hadn't spit in his neck.

****

We buried the hawk on the creekbank where everything seemed to have happened. The friends who had so recently helped Mother and the hawk celebrate their wedding now stood in stricken silence, watching us lower him into the ground.

Mother and I held each other tight as we went back home, making walking quite clumsy.

"He couldn't take not being able to live the way he was meant to live," she said. "Our home was just a final stop for him, a temporary shelter during the final days of his journey. The wilderness, that was where he belonged."

"Maybe he's happy now?" I asked hesitantly.

She didn't answer.

"Maybe he's free," I tried again, "in Heaven, flying above the clouds?"

Still nothing from her.

"Do you think so, Mother?"

"He realized that he couldn't last much longer," she finally said.

"So he knew he was going to die, Mother?"

"Probably. But you slamming the door on his head didn't help any."

I began to cry. All the bad things I had once felt about the hawk suddenly meant nothing. All that mattered was that I had hurt the hawk in many ways and now he was gone. And I had robbed Mother of her happiness.

"No, Billy, don't cry," Mother soothed. "He wouldn't want you to feel sad and guilty. Even though you soundly rejected him as a father, he realized it was just your way of trying to be free. He had put you in prison by taking your place as head of the family, just as we imprisoned him by trying to make him live like one of us." Her voice broke and she paused to compose herself.

"You let him out of prison in your own way. You have every reason for living, Billy, while he had very little. . ." At that point, she lost her voice and gave in to her tears.

After a soft crying jag, she dabbed at her eyes with a tissue and said, "I love you, Billy."

I hugged her even harder. "I love you too, Mother."

We held that mobile embrace for a long time, walking like conjoined twins toward the house. Then she gave a tiny laugh and said, "Listen to us." She wiped the last of her tears. "Let's go on home. We've got quite a mess to clean up."

"I'll help," I said.

"Gosh," she laughed. "Wasn't that banana thing a hoot!"

****

A few months later, Mother was driving to town when she ran over a Saint Bernard that darted out in front of the car. She assessed his injury, decided he would live, and brought him home. He slowly recovered at our farm under her care, although it was obvious he would never again be the slobbering, boisterous canine Nature had intended him to be.

One evening Mother giggled as she brushed his coat and rubbed his belly as he lay on his back, paws limp in the air. Something that smelled like God's death was baking in the oven. Suddenly the Saint Bernard cocked his head toward me.

"Billy, if I ever have the opportunity to father another litter of pups, I'd want my sons to be just like you. Now go outside and find me a nice bone. I don't care how many garbage cans you have to rifle through. And no chicken bones for me to choke on, goddam it." He winked at Mother and she tittered.

A thought skipped jaggedly through my head that once again I was being displaced in my own home. But another feeling welled up stronger. Commitment to family, I realized, was in itself a sort of freedom.

Later that night after Mother and Bernie had gone to bed, I sneaked out of my room and went alone to the hawk's grave. There was a beautiful crescent moon smiling sideways at me, and I felt spirits in the air.

"I promise I'll never use this again," I whispered as I lay my rifle down next to his neckstone. "And I'll be careful with Mother's new boyfriend, especially around doors. And most of all, I'll practice respect toward all living things, human and otherwise." I turned and started back to the house where my family was sleeping peacefully.

I hope I let you out of your cage, Stepfather, I thought as the night carried me toward home. *I'll never cage another animal as long as I live.*

Then, right under that gorgeous sliver of moon, I realized that the Saint Bernard would never again run free, that he was trapped in our house forever. All he had left was remorse—and me to take it out on. I thought of Mother's irritating giggle when she was with him.

I went back to the hawk's grave, picked up my rifle, and headed for home.

Printed in Poland
by Amazon Fulfillment
Poland Sp. z o.o., Wrocław

49309031R00129